FOOL ME TWICE

D0168522

The  line

Fool Me Twice
by Mandy Hubbard

Wish You Were Italian
by Kristin Rae

Not in the Script
by Amy Finnegan
(coming soon)

FOOL ME TWICE

An IF ONLY *novel*

Mandy Hubbard

BLOOMSBURY
NEW YORK LONDON NEW DELHI SYDNEY

SOMERSET CO. LIBRARY
BRIDGEWATER, N.J. 08807

Copyright © 2014 by Mandy Hubbard
All rights reserved. No part of this book may be reproduced or transmitted in any form
or by any means, electronic or mechanical, including photocopying, recording, or by any information
storage and retrieval system, without permission in writing from the publisher.

First published in the United States of America in May 2014
by Bloomsbury Children's Books
www.bloomsbury.com

Bloomsbury is a registered trademark of Bloomsbury Publishing Plc

For information about permission to reproduce selections from this book, write to
Permissions, Bloomsbury Children's Books, 1385 Broadway, New York, New York 10018
Bloomsbury books may be purchased for business or promotional use. For information on bulk
purchases please contact Macmillan Corporate and Premium Sales Department at
specialmarkets@macmillan.com

Library of Congress Cataloging-in-Publication Data
Hubbard, Amanda.
Fool me twice : an If only novel / Mandy Hubbard.
pages   cm
Summary: After a whirlwind summer romance, Landon broke up with Mackenzie and now,
working together again at Serenity Ranch and Spa, Mack and her best friend Bailey are
fantasizing about revenge when a fall gives Landon amnesia that has him thinking he and Mack
are still together.
ISBN 978-1-61963-230-1 (paperback) • ISBN 978-1-61963-229-5 (hardcover)
ISBN 978-1-61963-231-8 (e-book)
[1. Love—Fiction.   2. Dating (Social customs)—Fiction.   3. Health resorts—Fiction.]
I. Title.
PZ7.H856676Foo 2014   [Fic]—dc23   2013044565

Book design by Amanda Bartlett
Typeset by Westchester Book Composition
Printed and bound in the U.S.A. by Thomson-Shore Inc., Dexter, Michigan
2 4 6 8 10 9 7 5 3 1 (paperback)
2 4 6 8 10 9 7 5 3 1 (hardcover)

All papers used by Bloomsbury Publishing, Inc., are natural, recyclable products
made from wood grown in well-managed forests. The manufacturing processes
conform to the environmental regulations of the country of origin.

For Gracelynn and Elle

FOOL ME TWICE

CHAPTER ONE

"I love it when you act like guys are aliens," my best friend, Bailey, says, smirking as she tosses me a fluffy white towel.

I don't quite catch it before the burgundy *SR* monogram nails me in the eye and the towel smothers my face. I yank it off my head, no doubt ruining my quasi-punk-rock ponytail in the process. Or maybe messing it up enhances the effect. I'm not really sure because I'm still experimenting with my new look. "I don't act like they're *aliens*," I say, efficiently folding the towel and tucking it under the gleaming curve of the mahogany front desk. The subtle scent of lavender settles in my nose. I haven't yet figured out if the towels are washed in scented soap or if a magical fairy sprinkles lavender on them so each and every guest at Serenity Ranch will feel pampered.

Kidding. I don't think that way. But some of the guests seem to.

"Even if they're not from another planet, they're still impossible to predict." I tuck a few loose strands of electric-blue hair behind my ear. "I totally thought Landon would've said something by now."

"He's a dude, which makes him *insanely easy* to predict. He's moved on, Mack, and you should too." She shoves another towel onto the shelf under the desk, which looks like it's about to vomit them all back up. I don't know why they make us hide them anyway. This is a freakin' spa. Towels are a given.

I reach down for the last one in the basket. "Fine, maybe he's not an alien, but if I meant nothing, he'd treat me like everyone else, not give me the silent treatment. I bet he has ulterior motives for acting like this."

"Right. I'm sure it's step two in an elaborate fourteen-step process to woo you back."

I snort, then choke, my face heating as I end up in a raging coughing fit. Bailey curtsies, a move that somehow works in conjunction with her outfit. She's . . . vanilla, yet entirely perfect, in a khaki skirt that reaches the *exact* length required by Serenity Ranch and Spa, no more, no less, and a polo shirt with just enough preppie effect that she wouldn't be kicked off the resident golf course, either. Toss in a newsboy cap and some tasseled saddle shoes, she could totally be mistaken for one of *them.*

Meanwhile, I'm allowed to help in the spa, but technically I'm a lowly stable girl, hidden in the back aisles so as not to offend our wealthy clientele with the red and blue streaks in my hair. I don't know if the bright colors are expected to give them seizures, but I'm supposed to wear a hat if I'm going to be around the guests.

The thing is, the general manager—Mr. Ramsey—told us to

be prepared to dress "patriotically" for the ranch's annual Fourth of July extravaganza. It's the biggest weekend of the summer, but apparently I took it one step too far. Whatever. He proclaimed his patriotic expectations with a game-show-host sweep of his arms, all enthusiastic like. What was I supposed to do but take him *totally* seriously?

I should have gotten Employee of the Year, not exile. Until electric blue and fire-engine red wash out, I get to help Bailey in the morning, before the spa opens, then disappear to the sawdust and muck, and if I'm lucky, an afternoon of horseback riding. Wearing a helmet, of course, so as not to offend the delicate sensibilities of the upper class.

"I just wish I knew what he was thinking," I say, picking at a piece of glitter embedded in my nail polish so that I don't have to meet her eyes. "Is blue and red glitter polish too much, you think? I'm all about subtlety."

She ignores my sarcasm. "Why does he have to be thinking anything? The boy doesn't have two brain cells to rub together. He probably killed them all by getting kicked in the head by his gigantic horse."

It's weird, but I almost have the urge to defend him.

Almost.

She leans her hip against the counter, leveling an intense stare at me so that I have to look up as she says, "He wouldn't have dumped you if he had a triple-digit IQ."

Annnd, that's why Bailey is my best friend. "Thanks," I say, swinging open the nearby door and drop-kicking the laundry basket inside. "It's just that we've been here a week. How long is he going to ignore me?"

"You hardly talked all year at school. Why break the streak?"

I frown. "I don't know. I mean since this is where . . ."

My voice trails off. I don't have to complete the sentence. Bailey was here last year when Landon Falls and I had a whirlwind summer romance. She was there when I came home from our last date at two a.m. and told her I was in love with him. But unlike *Grease,* we returned to school and he totally did not break into a chorus about our summer loving in front of all his friends. Instead, he swept me under the rug and got back together with his ex-girlfriend.

The lame part is, this summer is practically a repeat. They broke up again a month ago, so now we're both single . . . and both here for another nine weeks. I keep thinking he's going to be trying for a romance redux. So far, nada.

"Like I said. Two brain cells. He probably forgot all about it." Her nose scrunches up as the words leave her mouth, and she realizes that wasn't exactly a comforting statement. I don't want to be forgotten and discarded.

I sigh. "Yeah, well, I guess I should go back to the barn with the other peasants."

Her grimace melts into a toothy grin. "Ah, yes, and tell me, just how *are* the accommodations in steerage?"

"The best I've ever seen," I say, playing along with her *Titanic* shtick. "Hardly any rats."

Bailey chuckles under her breath as she fishes a name tag out of the top drawer of the reception desk, pinning the shiny gold square to her polo. "What time will you be done?"

"Hmm, four or five? Depends on how many lessons we have today. I haven't seen this week's schedule yet."

"Awesome. I was thinking we could go into town. I'm totally out of toothpaste."

"You mean, *I'm* totally out of toothpaste," I correct, knowing Bailey never packs any toiletries because she prefers to use her suitcase space for cosmetics instead. It's a small price to pay for bunking with my best friend all summer with no parental supervision. "And that sounds good. I want some new sunglasses."

"You have sunglasses on top of your head."

"Yeah, ugly ones," I say, in my best *duh* voice. By now Bailey should know that a girl like me can never have too many accessories.

"Okay then. Strip mall it is!" she says, throwing her hands wide, fake enthusiasm dripping from her pores.

Right. Strip mall. The only downside to being this far removed from the real world. Even Target is a grueling trek worthy of its own major motion picture: *Mall Quest,* a two-hour epic! Many will try; few will survive!

I turn the key still sitting in the front door, toss it to Bailey, and then flip over the fancy little OPEN sign. "Have fun. Don't let the snobs bite."

"Don't let the horses condescend!"

I grin as I step into the sunshine.

Another summer at Serenity Ranch. The name is a misnomer at best. Maybe half the property is actually the ranch; the rest is a five-star spa and golf course. Even the "bunkhouses" scream luxury, with slate tile entries, twenty-foot ceilings, enormous antler chandeliers (totally fake, but one must maintain just the right mix of rustic and luxury), whirlpool tubs, and satellite television. The log bed frames look like authentic hand-sawed lumber assembled by an Amish guy, but they cost two thousand dollars and were imported from New York or something. New England. New Mexico? I can't remember. Last week a spoiled trust-fund brat broke one and pitched a fit when the front desk charged his credit card. I could hear him screaming from the barns.

I walk the dirt path toward the back stables, avoiding the concrete favored by our millionaire—and occasional billionaire—guests, since I'm not wearing the required hat to hide my hair. Beyond the barns are rolling, more-brown-than-green hills that hug the curve of the Columbia River.

People think Washington State is all greenery and never-ending rain. They envision the Emerald City, the Puget Sound, ferry boats, fresh salmon, and evergreen mountains . . . and maybe a few sparkly vampires playing baseball amid the lush forests. Most people have no idea that you only have to head eastbound on I-90 for about ninety minutes before you're over Snoqualmie Pass and the green mountaintops give way to rolling hills, and eventually even the sparse pines are replaced by crunchy tumbleweeds and dry rocks. If we didn't irrigate the fields, lawns, and golf courses, we'd have no grass at all.

Which isn't hard to believe, given the intensity of the heat beaming down at me at nine a.m. I round the final corner where the path is flanked on both sides by workers' cabins, and a familiar figure approaches.

"Hey, Mr. Ramsey," I call out, giving him a wave as I walk a little taller. There's something about the way he moves, the way he talks, that commands respect. His years of military service and ever-present buzz cut don't hurt.

"Mackenzie," he says, pausing under the shade of an old oak tree. "How are things going?"

"Good. Just got done helping Bailey in the spa," I say, jabbing a thumb back in the direction of the Empire of Towels. "Stall cleaning is up next."

"And how are the two new lesson horses working out?"

I nod my head. "They're calm as can be. I put two kids on them yesterday and they were perfect."

"Great. I trust that this summer will go as smoothly as last year?"

Sir, yes sir. "Absolutely."

"Excellent. Let me know if there is anything that should be addressed. I've got to get to the clubhouse."

And with that he's gone, and I can continue on my way to cottage 19, feeling like I just passed inspection. The tiny, rustic cabins at this end of the compound are part of the original ranch, back when this place was a little more authentic and catered to average people who wanted a genuine ranching experience. Now, they house the dozens of employees who don't live locally, and the guests stay in the new buildings.

I shove open the door and am greeted by our usual explosion of clothes, books, and DVDs. Rom coms for Bailey, and two dozen horror movies for me, which have spilled all over the floor. I haven't really had much time to watch any of them yet, mostly because Bailey hates scary movies, plus there are better things to do.

Last year, I spent all summer hung up on Landon. This summer, I'm determined to play the field, just like Bailey. A summer of boys and late-night swimming. A summer of shopping and music and riding horses.

Picking my way around the debris strewn about by Hurricane Bailey, I grab a Diet Coke from our mini-fridge and glance in the mirror.

I teased my hair when I got out of the shower, so my ponytail is a little higher than normal, and being clobbered with a towel this morning sort of helped the effect, as some strands now frame my face. I don't know if the average guy would find my style attractive, but I stand out, and I'd rather be unique than blend in with the masses.

I shrug at myself and head back out the door, following the path over a small knoll and then down, toward the back roll-up door to the stables, to where my duties—and Landon—await.

CHAPTER TWO

"I pledge allegiance, to the flag . . ."

I stiffen, my grip on the pitchfork, tightening so hard the wood bites into the still-developing calluses on my palms. The voice behind me is the very one I've waited to hear for the last week. . . . But he's *mocking me.*

I slice a glare in Landon's direction. He's standing in the entry to the empty stall, his lanky, all-too-muscular body a silhouette against the fluorescent fixture hanging behind him. The dust kicked up by my work swirls in the light hugging his body.

I wish I could make out his expression, to figure out if it's the same sneer he gave me that first day back at school last fall. When he broke my heart.

I smirk, saying, "Ha, ha, ha. You must think you're super clever."

"Actually, I do." He puts a hand to his heart. "You really wound my ego."

I roll my eyes. " 'No tears, please. It's a waste of good suffering.' "

He drops his hand back to his side. "Are you quoting *Hellraiser*?"

I blink. "Um, no?" I turn back to the pitchfork, hoping he buys it, and toss another scoop into the overflowing wheelbarrow. I should have emptied it already, but this is the last stall.

"Since when do you like classic horror movies?" His voice has that old familiar drawl to it, that same twang I loved when he whispered to me, his breath hot on my ear. His family is from Texas. They moved to Washington State six years ago, but he's never let go of the accent.

"Since when do you care what I like?" I scoop at a pile of manure near his toes, daring him to stand still as it slides dangerously close to his battered Justin cowboy boots. He doesn't move. "I mean, I was *just* getting used to the silent treatment."

"Meh, I got bored," he says.

Bored. I scowl. "I'm sure there's a *real* flag somewhere in desperate need of your allegiance."

I scoop up another forkful of soiled bedding. Maybe he thought he'd get away with just waltzing up, that I'd somehow forget what he did, like I'd fall at his feet at the first sign of his interest.

When I look up at him again, he hasn't budged, he's just chewing on his lip. He licks his lip, and for a second I forget I'm staring, thinking about how it felt when we'd kissed, when he'd traced his tongue across *my* lips. When he grins, I realize he's caught me.

Ugh. I should not be thinking of how good he is at kissing. Actually, scratch that. I should be thinking of how good he is at kissing *other girls.* That made it pretty easy to stay angry. Like he did in the halls the first day of school last fall. I wore this adorable Zac Brown Band T-shirt because he said they were his favorite band, and I was practically bursting with excitement to see him after a few days apart . . . and then I saw him, but it didn't go the way I'd pictured.

He was leaning in to kiss *her,* while I stood there dumbfounded. He knew exactly what he was doing because midway through their steamy makeout session, he saw me staring, a strange gleam in his eyes as he watched the way I unraveled. It was like he enjoyed watching me shatter, just like little boys love burning ants with magnifying glasses.

And it sucks to be the ant. I am *so over* being the ant.

"Nah, you're a little more . . . lively."

I snort, shaking my head. Lively. Yeah, I could show him lively.

"What?" he asks, crossing his arms and leaning against the doorway. The effort makes his muscles bulge. He probably practices the move in his mirror in the hopes of using it to ensnare his next summer fling.

I toss the pitchfork onto the heaping wheelbarrow. "Just leave me alone, okay?" I grab the cart's handle and yank.

But he doesn't move, and I back right up into him, our bodies colliding. Instead of stepping aside, he grabs my elbows to keep me from knocking him completely over, and then actually removes me from the stall and slides me into the aisle, like I'm a kitten that's run into his path.

Then he turns and easily pulls the overladen cart over the bump, onto the smooth cement of the aisle. The stall door screeches as he rolls it shut.

"I still have to put pellets in there," I start.

"I'll get it."

I stare at him, unwilling to believe he'd volunteer to take on even a tiny portion of my workload without wanting something in return. "Well, you just go zero to sixty in about five seconds, don't you?"

He flashes me a wolfish smile, the one that makes him seem half-dangerous, half-sexy. But now I know what really lurks beneath all those muscles and cowboy swagger, and his smile is no longer so attractive.

"What's that supposed to mean?" he asks, tipping the rim of his cowboy hat back far enough that I can see into his intense brown eyes. He's . . . irritated.

Good.

I narrow my own eyes and match his look. "The silent treatment, to mockery, to doing me favors," I say, ticking them off on my fingers. "Before you turned on the roller coaster, you could have at least warned me to keep my hands and feet in the car at all times."

He huffs. "Can't a guy do a girl a favor?"

"No." I laugh, and not in a pretty way. "Not you, anyway."

Dang. I had wanted to be aloof. Unaffected. I'm screwing it up.

He shrugs, totally unbothered by my visceral response. "Fine then. Do it yourself," he says. But he doesn't move out of my way or open the stall door either. Instead, his eyes sweep over my now-dirty polo shirt, down my legs, and then back up again before he smirks. "What's with the getup?"

I grit my teeth and check out my outfit. I'm in my Serenity Ranch polo, as required, along with my jean shorts, but I have lime-green leggings underneath, and my cowboy boots don't match any of my clothes—they're powder blue. It's like my outfit is a mullet—business on the top, party on the bottom.

"Can't wear plain old shorts in a saddle, you know that," I say, like he's being stupid. "It pinches."

"Right. And regular jeans would just be too . . ."

"Boring?" I say, throwing his words back at him.

"Uh-huh, and being a freak show—"

My anger explodes. "What do you want, Landon? Hurting me last year wasn't enough and now you've gotta waltz in here and insult me?"

Crap. I wasn't planning to admit how much he hurt me. I'm ruining all of this. Bailey's going to laugh me out of our cabin later.

In response, he crosses his arms and waits as if he was the one to ask the question and he's expecting an answer, but I have nothing else to say. And then he just shrugs and walks away, whistling an all-too-familiar tune.

Oh say can you seeeeeeee.

Ugh.

CHAPTER THREE

An hour later, I'm tightening the cinch of an old Crates barrel saddle, the one I adore because it doesn't creak and squeak like the newer ones used by the guests. I step back, leaving the stirrup still hooked over the horn, and wait thirty seconds, watching the mare's stomach.

She exhales and I reach in to tighten the cinch. "Gotcha."

"Uh, hi."

I whirl around to find a guy in faded overalls and a snug red T-shirt, unfolding a scrap of paper. He's probably twenty or so, with a mop of curly brown hair barely contained by an SR-monogrammed hat.

"Hi," I say, dropping the stirrup back down on Zoey's saddle. "Looking for someone?"

"Sorta?" He scrunches up his nose. "A horse, actually."

"Really?" I glance over his outfit again. It's a little more mechanic than cowboy.

"Well, not the horse exactly, but the stall. For"—he glances at the paper again—"Musa."

Realization dawns. "Ah. You must be the handyman." I extend my hand. "Mack."

"Like the truck?" He smiles and it's a little goofy, kind of lopsided.

"Like Mackenzie," I say. "I'll show you where the stall is. We moved Musa out to the corral when his door broke."

"Cool," he says, picking up the toolbox at his feet and following me down the cement aisle. "I'm Adam, by the way."

"Worked here long?" I ask, running my fingers along the series of steel rods comprising the stall fronts. Most of the stalls are empty, the horses either being ridden or relaxing out in the corrals with Musa.

"A week, actually. I'm just doing it for the summer. I'm on break from University of Washington."

"Oh cool. The summer temps kinda stick together, you know."

"Why? Should I be expecting the permanent employees to give me a hard time?"

I shrug. "I mean, not really, but they've got all year to really gel, you know? They can be a little clique-ish."

"Oh."

"Yeah, uh, anyway . . . what are you studying at UW?"

"I'm premed," he says, swinging the toolbox as he walks. I blink as his words sink in, and he must catch my reaction.

His smile is sheepish. "I know, I don't really look like a doctor. I'm hoping that will come later."

"Sorry, I didn't . . ."

He waves my apology away. "Nah, I get it. This is more me," he says, motioning to his handyman getup.

"I was kind of thinking one of the *Super Mario* brothers," I say. "What with those overalls and red shirt. You just need some big white gloves and a ridiculous mustache."

He laughs. "And a brother named Luigi."

"Exactly."

The smile melts away and he gets a faraway look. "His name is Louis, actually. I'm half Italian. Dad's a contractor, so that's how I picked up the skills for this gig. Let me tell you, he is *thrilled* that all his forced child labor has readied me for such a glamorous summer job."

I giggle. He's kind of goofy, in a way that reminds me of my cousin. "If it makes you feel any better, I have exactly zero qualifications to be anything other than a barn minion."

He takes in the stalls and horses surrounding us, as if trying to decide how much my job sucks. "Do you hate it?"

"It's pretty awesome, actually," I say, pausing to touch the soft, velvety nose of a palomino yearling. "I mean I just got to the ranch last week, but I was here last summer too."

"Well hey, if you came back, it can't be all bad."

I walk another dozen feet. "Anyway, this is the stall." I point to the door, at the spot where the roller has pulled out from the wood, causing the whole thing to sit crookedly. "I kind of broke it yesterday."

He wiggles the door. "Do you turn into the Incredible Hulk when you're angry?"

"Maybe," I say. "I have to get out to the ring, though. I've got a lesson starting in a few minutes. If you need help finding your way around this place, let me know."

"Sure. And thanks."

I leave him there, surveying the damage, and return to my horse. I unclip the cross ties and put her halter around her neck. Then I grab the bridle and slip it over her nose, sliding the bit into her mouth and pushing the headstall up over her ears.

"Alrighty, let's go."

On my way out, I grab a helmet and snap it into place. It's one of the few conditions of my working here. Mom wouldn't let me within a ten-yard radius of a horse if I didn't swear I'd wear one at all times, and Dad is the sort to back up any decision she makes. I didn't bother telling them about how Mr. Ramsey has that whole cover-thy-bizarre-hair-up-in-the-presence-of-guests expectation. Actually, I haven't even told them I dyed my hair to begin with. I kinda figure it'll be back to normal before I see them again.

It's not like I'm *actually* a freak show or anything. I don't wear goth makeup or combat boots. I don't spout Shakespeare or invent weird crap in my bedroom. I'm not a social leper, either. Bailey and I have our own clique of friends back home, and maybe we're not A-listers or class presidents or anything, but we're comfortable in the middle ground.

I just like clothes. At one point I considered getting into fashion, but then I visited Washington State University on a tour of colleges and fell in love, so I settled on a graphic design degree instead.

Last year, when I met Landon, I was like a tamer version of this. Jeans with a neon-pink tank and bangles, for instance. Maybe I've taken it too far for his tastes.

Not that I care, obviously.

I listen contentedly to the familiar *clip-clop* rhythm as Zoey, the chestnut with the big blaze, follows me through the barn doors and out into the sunshine. It's gotta be pushing ninety already, and it's only one o'clock. Bailey and I are so totally hitting up the river later.

I pull Zoey to the side of the entry, then stop, tossing her reins over her neck. " 'Atta girl. We won't work too hard today, promise."

Officially, my title is "lessons coordinator." The real instructor sits in the middle of the arena, calling out commands. Mostly, my job is to supervise it all, coming up alongside the riders who are having trouble and giving them pointers. It ends up more like a babysitting job, keeping the younger or inexperienced riders from losing control or getting too scared.

"Every guest must feel they've been given individual attention," as Mr. Ramsey says. It doesn't matter if they're eight years old and won't be filling out the comment card anytime soon. Marshall, the actual barn supervisor, doesn't really give a crap about the guests. He's more concerned about the horses. He's been at the ranch for, like, eighty million years, though, so it kind of comes with being a decades-long ranch hand.

I nod at the guy manning the gate, riding through as he swings it open and Zoey steps into the dusty arena. It's watered between every forty-minute lesson, but it won't take long for the dirt to kick up and coat us all like we've been tossed around in a bag of Shake 'n Bake.

I swing along the railing, which is still empty, as the riders will show up at the last minute when the ranch hands bring out their horses. Years and years ago, before this place went yuppie, the guests would have learned to tack up their own horses. Now we do it for them, and they show up at the arena and climb aboard.

I circle the arena a couple of times at a walk, enjoying the easy sway of my horse. It's amazing how quickly I settle back into horses after nine months away. I took lessons every week for five years, convinced someday my mom was going to sell our little rambler and buy a farm or something, but she never did. Doesn't every little girl want her own horse? But it was not to be. So now I stick to the summer at Serenity Ranch, riding whatever horse is available, which thankfully often means Zoey, my favorite.

I pick up a jog for a few laps, and then an easy lope, and I lose myself in the rhythm of it, sliding slightly in my saddle with each stride.

When I round the bend, the gate opens, and I frown at the sight of Landon leading a giant paint gelding into the ring. The same paint he hauled here last year and rode all summer. Unlike me, he *does* live on acreage. Not a massive farm or anything, but enough so that he has his own horse and a small arena, and around school people know him and his reputation, know he rodeos on the weekends.

"Whoa," I say, leaning back and picking up the reins. Zoey executes a perfect sliding stop. "What are you doing in here?"

Landon's bright eyes give him away. He enjoys my irritation. "I'm teaching today."

"Where's Tyler?" I ask, shielding my eyes from the sun.

He smirks. "Indisposed."

"What does that even mean?"

"He fell out of the hayloft," he says, arranging the reins over the gelding's neck, turning his back to me. "Broke his leg."

A sick feeling thickens in my stomach. "When is he going to be back?"

"August . . . ish?"

I grit my teeth. "So what, I'm going to be paired up with you for the next six weeks?"

He grins, and I want to stab him with a spork. " 'This is no dream! This is really happening!' " he says, but his voice is different, the Texan drawl completely gone.

I narrow my eyes as his words ring in my ear. "Isn't that from *Rosemary's Baby*?"

"See?" he says. "I called it. You totally like horror movies." He puts the toe of his broken-in brown boot into the stirrup and easily swings aboard. He settles into the saddle, and I try not to notice the way his worn-in Wranglers hug his thighs, knowing it's nothing more than a pretty candy shell on a rotten piece of garbage. He gathers the reins loosely in his hand. "It's like we're soul mates or something," he says, glancing up to meet my eyes.

I glare. "You knew about it this morning, didn't you?"

"Yes. It was obvious. I mean, only a true aficionado would quote *Hellraiser*. I can't believe I watched so many crappy blockbusters with you last year. I thought that's what you wanted."

"I thought that's what *you* were into! You're the one who suggested all those dumb Johnny Depp movies! And I'm not talking about the movie thing anyway. I meant about Tyler. You knew this morning."

"Maybe," he says, his expression passive.

"Wow, you're a piece of work," I mutter, then raise my voice. "So that's why you decided to talk to me. Smooth things over so I wouldn't be trouble for you."

The clouds shift, the sun intensifying along with my annoyance.

"Come on now," he says, grinning to show me I'm not so far off base. "Would I really be that conniving?"

"Yeah. You would."

I turn Zoey around, forgetting that she began her life as a reining horse, and she spins so hard I'm dangerously close to slipping off. I right myself and lope away from him, pleased I got the last word and embarrassed he's already getting the best of me.

I slow to a walk once I'm across the arena, and Zoey half snorts, half sighs. Movement catches my eye, and I watch as the first string of horses is led out, two at a time, by three other ranch hands, knowing the guests will soon follow.

Once they arrive, I'll have to play nice.

I'm not sure how I'll manage.

CHAPTER FOUR

I frown, staring into the mirror at a pair of Wranglers that Bailey talked me into trying on at a local western supply store.

"They're really plain," I call out, over the dressing room door.

"That's the point." She's on the other side of the divider, trying on a patterned red, white, and blue western button-up, presumably to wear at the Independence Day rodeo.

"The point is to look plain?" I ask, making a face at myself in the mirror.

"If you want to be allowed to work with me in the spa, you gotta blend," she says. "Isn't your hair a big enough fashion statement? If you must stand out, wear an ugly belt or something with them."

"Oh, thanks!" I say. She loves to jokingly refer to my fashion sense as ugly, atrocious, hideous, or a combination thereof, but

I've caught her trying on the occasional piece. "Besides, you're not even allowed to wear jeans in the spa."

"Jeans are step one. Stay in the stable and maybe fly under the radar for a week, and then we put you in khakis and see if Mr. Ramsey lets you stay. The spa would be way more fun if you were working with me."

I chew on my lip, not telling her that I actually prefer the horses—at least when I'm riding. I could do without mucking the stalls. But the stable is like a different world than where she works. I fit in there. Besides, the jeans may be plain, but they aren't actually that bad. They're snug, a deep indigo, and boot-cut to accommodate my usual barnyard footwear.

"But if I buy these, Landon's going to think I did it because of what he said today."

Dead silence. I dust a few pieces of lint off the butt of the jeans, twisting around to see how they look from the back.

The dressing room door flies open, bouncing off the wall, and I jump into the air, frantically covering my body before remembering I'm fully clothed.

"You talked to him?"

"Yeah. First in the barns, where he saluted my hair. And then we had to work together for three hours in the arena. He's going to be the instructor this summer." I grimace. "I'm practically his assistant."

"AND?" she says, clearly frustrated. "How'd the convo go?"

"You don't want to know."

"I don't?" she asks, crossing her arms.

I sigh. "Let's just say I fantasized about knocking him off that high horse of his."

"Literal or figurative?"

"Both," I say, nodding emphatically.

"Well, at least you guys are talking, right? Now you can remember what an arrogant jerk he is and move on." And then Bailey gets this ridiculous look in her eye, and she struggles to hold back a smile. "And speaking of moving on, I kind of thought you could use those jeans so as not to scare off the Trenton brothers."

"Wait, what?"

"They're coming over at eight."

I check the giant purple plastic watch on my wrist. "It's going to take us that long to get back to the ranch!"

"I know, but a lady is allowed to arrive fashionably late."

"I'm pretty sure real ladies don't invite brothers to come over to their cabins for romantic trysts," I say, reaching out to check the price tag dangling from Bailey's sleeve. "Thirty bucks is way too much for this tragedy."

"I know, right?" she says, shrugging. "But anyway, real ladies don't wear miniskirts either. I'm inventing this crap as I go along."

"Oh, like a trashy-lady hybrid?"

She grins. "Exactly. I'm like Nicki Minaj meets Kate Middleton."

I roll my eyes and go back to the mirror. "So . . . you *actually* want me to buy these jeans because the guys are coming over, and you don't think either of them will give me the time of day in an oversized David Bowie T-shirt and patterned tights?"

Bailey fake-gags. "You do not own a David Bowie shirt."

"I do. My sister bought it for me as a joke, and I happen to think it's so ugly it swung back around to being cute."

"Ew." Bailey actually recoils at that, as if the shirt might pop up from underneath the changing bench and attack her. "Yeah, definitely not that. So go buy the jeans."

"I *have* jeans, you know."

"Yeah," she says, in her best *duh* voice. "A pair with seventeen holes in them—I counted—and the pair with pink Sharpie marker art."

"Or I could wear that fifties eyelet dress," I say, eyeballing the jeans again.

"They're cowboys, not madmen," she says, with a raised brow. I've forgotten how many rules there are when shopping with Bailey. "Stick with the jeans. Trust me. You said you wanted to have fun this summer! It starts tonight."

"All right, all right. I'll get them. But you're buying the toothpaste."

"Deal. Because in two hours, we're both going to be glad we have minty-fresh breath."

CHAPTER FIVE

I'm slumped into an armchair in the corner of our living room, my feet propped up on the matching footstool as I watch *Pitch Perfect*, the oscillating fan blowing in my direction the only thing saving me from the heat.

I tried to talk Bailey into watching the latest incarnation of *Texas Chainsaw Massacre*, but she said it would kill the mood. Instead, her movie selection is doing nothing to keep my mind away from the sounds of Bailey flirting with Trenton brother number one. I know he's Trenton brother number one because number two deigned not to show up tonight, and now I'm in serious third-wheel mode. I also know it's flirting—even though I can't hear exactly what she's saying—based on the fact that she's giggling every 2.4 seconds.

I'm trying not to be totally insulted by being stood up, but I can't help it, and it's totally soured my mood. Maybe if we'd picked a movie Bailey hasn't forced me to watch a dozen times this year alone, I could pay more attention to the story and less to the empty beanbag chair next to me.

Bailey giggles again and shoves his shoulder, and Trenton brother number one grabs her hand, then makes this whole grandiose gesture of kissing her knuckles, and I think I might actually die from saccharine overdose.

"I'm going out!" I say, jumping up and striding through the front door before they have a chance to respond. Once outside, I'm not sure what to do with myself. I'd be a total creeper if I just sat on the porch swing, listening to them flirt.

Sighing, I sit down on the edge of a creaky step, pulling on my powder-blue cowboy boots from this morning, then sliding my jeans over the outside of the boots. Stupid Wranglers. I should be wearing something cuter, more me and less Bailey. I tried to wear my *Nightmare Before Christmas* T-shirt, but Bailey said it was too morbid. Instead, she made me wear one of her tank tops, a white one with a huge silver horseshoe, convinced it would be like a homing beacon and Trenton brother number two would stare into my chest and be hypnotized.

Too bad he'd have to show up to do that. Whatev, didn't need him anyway. The cute one—the blond—is the one currently taking up residence on our couch, and Bailey had dibs on him, since she invited them over. Not that his brother's not cute too, but he totally has a snaggletooth.

Who needs a snaggletooth in her life, anyway? Not me. Totally not me.

I stand and wander down the path, not really sure where I'm going or what I want to do. Or what I really want in general, for this summer. I thought I was going to come here and be just like her, having a blast and not caring about the repercussions. I guess I'm more of a lover than a flirter.

Or maybe it's just being here and seeing Landon and remembering what it was like to fall in love that makes it impossible to ignore those feelings. Makes it impossible to just be casual and flirty.

Stupid Landon and his stupid smile.

I pass by the last cabin in our row and wave to a pair of cowboys playing poker on a tiny folding table. One of them nods at me, but the other is too busy staring at his hand of cards. I've never really figured out if they like me or just put up with me every summer, but they seem to respect Landon. Maybe they're more into arrogant jerks than totally kick-butt, awesome girls.

I walk down to the stable, but the doors are shut, and I don't particularly feel like going inside and lighting up the place and remembering just how alone I am. The stables are so quiet at night.

So I bypass them and opt for a nice walk, strolling the dirt pathways past the spa, following the curve of the golf course. The *whoosh-whoosh-whoosh* sound of the sprinklers kicks in, ensuring our pampered guests have perfectly green . . . golf greens.

In the late dusk light, the air is warm but not overwhelming, and the crickets around me sing as I leave the faint glow of the ranch behind, cresting a small hill. Below me, the Columbia River flows, wide and slow. Downstream a few miles, the water is surrounded by enormous cliffs carved out by glaciers. But here, near the ranch, the banks are little more than a gentle slope, the brown landscape turning green and then muddy. In one area, the bank curves in, creating a side pool, a perfect swimming hole you can only see once you're right on top of it.

It's cooled off considerably, yet I'm sweating by the time I make it to the river. I'm not dumb enough to swim alone, but maybe I'll kick off my boots and roll up my pant legs and sit on the old log near the shore. Just enough to cool down a bit, enjoy the feeling of the water on my legs.

As I round the boulder everyone uses to hang their towels and clothes on, though, all thoughts of the water fly out the window.

Landon's standing there with this back to me, staring into the darkness, shirtless.

Shirtless.

The muscles of his back are well defined, pulled tight over his shoulders as he fiddles with what must be his ever-present belt buckle, a big silver and gold shiny thing he wears all summer long.

"Don't you know you get fired if you swim alone?" I say, before I can stop myself. As if he ever cared about anything found in the employee handbook. It's loosely enforced, if that, and Landon always did play by his own rules.

It's like he knew I was coming, because he doesn't startle, he just yanks on the buckle, making the buttery leather snake out of the belt loops. Then he turns around and gives me that wolfish smile, his teeth glinting in the moonlight.

"Does it look like I care?"

My mouth goes dry. His chest is smooth and tan, and the top button of his Wranglers is unbuttoned.

"You never really did," I say, not sure if I'm talking about me or the rules.

"That's where you're wrong," he says, and I can tell he's not talking about the rules either. He swallows, then he grits his teeth, the muscles in his jaw jumping. "I did care. A lot."

Did. Past tense. Why can't I feel that way? These thoughts, feelings, they should be past tense. He wasn't even man enough to dump me at the end of the summer. Instead he just started making out with someone new.

I should be in the cabin with Bailey, sucking face with a Trenton brother and his crooked tooth.

"You have a funny way of showing it," I say instead.

He tips his head to the side, studying me with an unreadable expression. "I never claimed to be perfect."

I don't know what he means by that. His imperfection was dropping me the second his ex was willing to take him back. Yeah, I always wanted to be a Band-Aid for a guy who couldn't hold himself together after getting dumped. "You were really going to swim alone?" I ask, trying to get the subject back on track. "That's dangerous." I sound stupid.

"Well, then, I'm lucky I don't have to now," he says, and with that he slips his jeans over his hips, revealing the royal-blue boxer-briefs that had been peeking out of his waistband.

My mouth goes dry. "I'm not swimming with you."

"That's a shame; what if I drown?"

"Then good riddance," I say. "It's your funeral." I turn around, depressed that I seem to be getting run out of every safe haven at the ranch, and annoyed that every conversation with him gets so intense so fast. I've made it two steps when I sense he's closer now, and I have no time to react before his hands are on my hips, and he's twirled me around and tossed me over his shoulder.

"Put me down, you idiot!" He's half-naked, and from my perspective all I can see and feel is his bare skin as it curves down to his backside, to where flesh meets his boxers. His skin is hot to the touch, and his step is jarring as he walks toward the river.

"I swear to God if you throw me in . . ."

And then he's dropping me and I'm on my feet again, but this time my hands are on his arms and the heels of my boots sink into the mud at the edge of the bank.

He smirks down at me, and I have to crane my neck to meet his eyes. "I'll give you one minute to kick those boots off and strip down or you'll go in fully clothed."

"I am *not* going skinny-dipping with you."

"It's a bra and underwear. Nothing I haven't seen before," he says, his lips curling into that stupid smile, the one that makes me think of kissing him. "As I recall, you did this quite willingly last year."

"Oh, so you *do* remember," I say, shoving his chest.

He doesn't even flinch. "Thirty seconds and those god-awful boots of yours are getting the river treatment."

" 'I will not be threatened by a walking meatloaf.' "

"American Werewolf in Paris," he rattles off, without even pausing to think. "And stop distracting me. You're not getting out of this."

I gawk at him. "You are *not* throwing me in this river."

"Fifteen seconds."

Dang it all, I know he means it, that he's not above tossing me in like a rat and ruining my boots. In an instant, I yank them off my feet. I look into his eyes to see if he's still serious, and then grit my teeth and yank my shirt over my head, feeling a little thrill as his gaze travels downward. I can't help but wonder if his cheeks feel as hot as my own.

Then, without taking my eyes off of his, with the most defiant look I can muster, I yank off my jeans, happy that at least I wore cute red bikini underwear and a matching bra.

But they were for snaggletooth, not heartbreaker.

Then without a word I turn away from him, walk into the river, and dive under the surface, hoping the water will conceal the sounds of my pounding heart. When I break the surface, I smooth my hair out of my face, wondering how well the red, blue, and blond go with the river and the moonlight.

I splash in his direction, although it's fruitless because he's still on shore. "You're a real jerk, you know that?" I call out over the sounds of the water, watching him as he wades in, so slowly it's like he's doing it on purpose, wanting me to anticipate him.

It's the smooth behavior I fell for so easily last year. A well-honed, practiced routine aimed at reeling me in and then moving on in an instant.

"You know you came here to swim," he says. "I just made sure your pride didn't get in your way."

"*My* pride? I don't think it's *my* pride that's the problem," I say, treading water, kicking slightly away from him as he comes closer, the water lapping at his shoulders.

I want him to fix it.

I want the last year to disappear.

I want it to be the summer I let myself fall for him. I want him to have a reason for everything he did to me. I want him not to have used me the way he did, as a placeholder when he missed his real girlfriend.

But no matter how much I want it, it won't be true. I can't be stupid and fall for the same old ploy all over again. Even if he is breathtaking in the moonlight, I can't let him get that close.

"You're the one intent on fighting. I tried to be nice this morning, help you with your stalls, and you went into attack mode."

"We've both been here over a week and you didn't talk to me until you knew we'd be forced to work together. I call that an ulterior motive."

"So maybe that *is* what convinced me to finally talk to you again," he says, standing still on the river bottom as he stares at me, his eyes hooded in shadows. "But it doesn't make it an ulterior motive. It just means I didn't have the guts last week, and I finally forced myself."

Him not having the guts to talk to a girl is preposterous. He really does know how to manipulate people. "I think you've spent too much time on the ranch, because you're full of crap."

He laughs, and God, is it sexy. "Can't you just cut me a little break? Have a nice swim for old times' sake?"

Images of the two of us last summer, as we kissed for the first time, right here in the swimming hole under the light of the stars, flood my vision. I force the thoughts away. "If you hadn't dumped me in favor of that *perfect* little girlfriend of yours, it wouldn't be old times."

"Jealous?" he asked, something flashing in his eyes, something I can't read in the moonlight.

My laugh is sad and bitter. "I can't do this, Landon. I can't. I'm not going to be there for you every time you're lonely. I can't put myself through that again."

I lean forward, meaning to swim to shore but he grabs me, pulling me up against him. My feet barely brush the bottom if I put down my tippy-toes, but he has a good eight inches on me, so his feet are firmly on the ground.

"It's not like that."

I shove his chest and he loosens his hold so that I'm not pressed up against the length of him, every inch of his legs, his hips, his abs, hot on mine . . . but he doesn't completely release me. He has no right to be so touchy-feely. I'm not his anymore.

"What is it like then, huh? What did you think we were *last year*? I've been waiting all these months for some kind of magical answer, so why don't you give it to me?"

He swallows, then opens his mouth as if to give me the answer I want, but he just snaps it shut again.

"Don't think I don't remember how it felt to be swept aside like yesterday's garbage. I deserve better than that, and I won't let you do it again." I draw in a shaky breath, desperate to rein myself in, to find the composure I thought I could maintain around him. I swallow down the feelings growing in my throat. "Just answer me one question," I say.

"Of course," he says, and by the softness in his voice I almost believe I'm getting to him, almost believe he regrets what he did to me.

Tears, blast them, glimmer in my eyes, and I pray he thinks it's just splashed water. "When you said good-bye to me that last day at the ranch . . . when I told you . . ." I stop for a second, hating what I'm about to say, before taking a deep breath and surging forward. "When I told you that I loved you and you kissed me, did you know even then that you were going to choose her?"

His arms slacken more, and it's all the response I need. I shove myself away, the water sloshing up around my shoulders.

And in the moonlight, he says the word I'm waiting for. "Yes."

CHAPTER SIX

"I'll kill him. With my bare hands, I'll kill him," Bailey says as we sit on the top rail of the arena, our ankles hooked underneath the pipe railing one row down.

"You have my permission," I say drily.

"What is he doing? Does he get some sick pleasure from toying with you?"

I blow out a long, slow sigh, brushing back a loose strand of blue hair sticking to the sweat on my temple. "Heck if I know. How am I going to hold it together? I already have PTSD from last summer."

"That's it!" she says, brightening. "We treat this like war, and we use an IED."

"Whoa, I'm not trying to blow him up. And I don't even know where you'd find the materials for that."

"I mean, not him, obviously," she says, slapping my knee. "Maybe his truck. He's kind of in love with it."

"Um, maybe we can come up with a plan that doesn't involve a felony," I say, fighting a smirk.

"Yeah, yeah. Party pooper," she says, waving me away. "This blows. I can't believe he's acting like you're going to be a door-mat and just be his summer hookup again."

I purse my lips, nodding. "Yeah, that pretty much seems to be what he's thinking."

"What a jerk."

I laugh. I'm glad Bailey is my friend, here to think dark thoughts with me. She'd totally make a voodoo doll of his hair if I had any, and she'd stay up late so we could invent some freaky ceremony to curse him.

"Hey, Mack," a voice calls out. I turn around to see Adam pushing a big wheelbarrow with shovels in it.

"Oh, hey, Adam," I say. "Looking for mushrooms?"

"You know it," he says, chuckling. "I'm hoping for fire-breathing superpowers."

"That's totally from the fire flower plant thingy, not the mush-rooms, the mush—"

Bailey elbows me, hard, in the stomach.

I wince and elbow her back. "Uh, anyway, have you met my friend Bailey? She works in the spa."

"Nope. Hi, Bailey," he says, reaching out his hand. She shakes it.

"Hey, yourself," she says, holding his hand for a moment lon-ger than necessary.

He drops the handshake and turns to me. "I gotta go fix a creaky step on cabin twenty-seven, but I'll let you know if I see any mushrooms along the way."

"Perfect," I say, and we exchange awkward little waves as he walks away.

"What the heck was all that talk of mushrooms?"

"Uh, I might have told him he looked like Super Mario."

"You did not!"

"Did too."

"You are so weird," Bailey says.

"Am not." I twist back around so we're facing the ring again.

"Yeah, you definitely are. But he's super cute, don't you think?" she says.

I snicker. "I guess."

"You don't think so?"

I shrug. "He's okay. Not really my type."

"Good. I call dibs," Bailey says. "Anyway, back to the task at hand. I think we should at least swap out Landon's shampoo with Nair or something," she says, drumming her fingers on her knee.

"His hair is his greatest asset, after all," I agree. "All thick and blond and spiky or whatever. Gives him that whole tall, handsome vibe."

"Really?" She stops drumming her fingers, genuine surprise in her eyes. "Because I thought he'd be such a good kisser, with those full lips of his. . . ."

"Don't go there," I say, shaking away any memory of *that* variety. "So not discussing it."

"Fine. It's not like you have a scale for comparison, anyway," she says, pursing her lips and nodding in a strangely solemn way, like it's really important to rate his kissing ability.

"Please tell me you don't have a scale," I say, sitting up again and fanning myself with my hand, though it does nothing but make me even hotter.

She grins, that familiar wicked gleam in her eye. "Sure. I

like to know how great a guy is on a scale between Trevor Green-
wood and Patrick Burrows."

"Patrick Burrows?" I ask, thinking of the boy from my home-
room class, the one who spent the whole time creating anagrams
from SAT words. "Really?"

"Yep. Best kisser by far."

I shudder. "I can't believe we're best friends."

"I know, you're so lucky," she says, and we both laugh, knocking shoulders. Then she clears her throat. "Oh, speak of the devil."

"Patrick Burrows?" I ask, shielding my eyes from the sun to
see in the direction of Bailey's nod. "Oh."

"Is his horse always that hyper?"

Storm is dancing at the end of the reins, but Landon just
maintains his solid grip and walks as if it's no big deal that a
thousand-pound horse is hopping around like a bunny on crack.
"Yeah, pretty much. He's got his roping saddle on and Storm
knows it. He's a total hothead for roping."

"Oh."

"Should we bail?" I ask. "I mean, I don't know the rules of
engagement. Without the aid of explosives or whatever."

"First, no, you do not let him run you off, and second, *dude*,
explosives! We could blow up his junk."

I laugh. "I wish."

We don't move from the fence panel, which thankfully is
at the far corner of the arena, one of the few spots with shade.
Another rider on a horse appears, as do a couple of other guys
who walk over to the chutes.

"He must be practicing for the upcoming rodeo," I say. It's
not really a high-stakes rodeo—more of an expo, really, in which

some of the locals and the hands run through the usual events. It's kinda silly, since they don't get too competitive about it, but it's easily the biggest draw of the summer for our guests. A real live rodeo, right outside their log cabins.

The cabins are already sold out, which makes this lunch break all the more important. Bailey and I have been working like crazy all morning, and I'm not eager to go back to work twenty minutes earlier than I have to.

As for the rodeo, I'm in it too. I'm running barrels. I'm not any good at it, but neither are the other two girls, so the guests never seem to know the difference. Half of them think that a fast lope and a gallop are the same thing, and who am I to point it out? Everyone gets a bonus at the end of the summer if the comment cards are 95 percent satisfactory or better, so we've learned to fake it.

There's a commotion at the other end of the arena, and it's obvious the guys are loading the chutes, because I see a white-faced steer pop into view as he crow-hops inside the little box. Landon climbs aboard his horse with his usual practiced ease, settling into the saddle before turning away and starting his warm-up.

Either he doesn't notice us or he's ignoring me, because he stays at the other end of the arena, trotting in lazy, large circles rather than hugging the rail and coming all the way around, to where Bailey and I are sitting.

"He's totally ignoring you," Bailey says, voicing my thoughts.

"Good," I say. "I really don't want to talk to him."

"We can't possibly nail him with ball-exploding devices all the way over here," she says.

"A real tragedy," I say, smiling. Somehow when she's by my side I feel less like I'm about to come undone.

"Why'd he toss his rope?" she asks, gesturing to where he hooked it over a post.

"Maybe he's practicing steer wrestling first," I say. "It's his best event."

"Because he's just psycho enough to hurtle himself from a horse at a full gallop and hope that the cow will break his fall?" Bailey says.

"Pretty much."

I watch Landon as he circles around one more time, then slows to a walk and heads over to the big boxed area. Then he turns Storm, who is prancing like it's his job, and backs him up into the box.

The horse's muscles quiver and he snorts, trembling with excitement. The other rider—the guide horse—backs into the box on the opposite side of the chute. This guy's job is just to run in a straight line, ensuring the steer has to run directly to the other side of the arena.

I was right, it's steer wrestling. The same configuration as team roping, but neither of them has a rope.

Despite my loathing of all things Landon, I can't help the jump in my pulse as he nods, his cowboy hat bobbing to indicate he's ready.

A guy on the ground yanks a lever and the steer bursts from the chute, and Storm jumps forward, going from a dead stop to a full-blown gallop in a single stride. The rider on the opposite side of the steer leaps forward, and the two gallop ahead, the steer between them, looking tiny in comparison to the giant horses.

Halfway down the arena, Landon lets go of the reins, leaning in low. He slides from the saddle, positioned just right. . . .

And then the steer makes an odd little hop of sorts . . . and Landon's sliding down . . .

Until he slams into the ground.

CHAPTER SEVEN

I'm in the dirt and running toward Landon before I even process what I'm doing. The other rider has his back to Landon, loping after Storm in order to keep the horse from running too long and letting the reins droop low enough to catch in the horse's hooves. The guy is clearly unaware that Storm's rider is lying completely immobile in the dirt. Meanwhile the steer, unscathed, trots back the way it came.

I slide to my knees when I get closer, my stomach climbing into my throat as I realize his eyes are shut and he's not moving.

"Landon!" I say, afraid to touch him. His hat landed back at least a dozen feet, and his arm is sort of jacked underneath him. *Stupid, stupid boy.* He should have followed the helmet rule, but he's too busy trying to be one of the ultra-tough cowboys.

"Landon!" I reach out to touch his shoulder, but then I stop, unsure if that would make it worse. What are the rules with falls? What's more important, spinal injury or making sure he's breathing? It's gotta be the breathing, right?

Bailey falls to her knees beside me just as a few people call out, followed by the clanging of the gate and footsteps as the other guys flood toward us.

Landon's eyelids flutter, but he keeps his eyes shut as he moans, shifting just enough that he's not lying on his arm anymore. "Oh thank God," I say, finally touching his shoulder. "Landon, wake up."

I exchange a worried glance with Bailey and then Landon's eyes open, but he's blinking, again and again and again, like he's having trouble focusing. I lean in, planning to take his pulse, but when my fingers touch his throat his eyes find mine, and I freeze.

"What happened?" he asks, his voice a little breathless and pained.

"Um . . ." Is it bad to tell him he just crash-landed on his head? Would that be too jarring or something?

"Be honest, babe."

I recoil, my fingers leaving the warmth of his throat as I look up at Bailey's furrowed brow and parted lips.

"Uh," I say, and then swallow. "You just kind of bit it while you were steer wrestling. Like, totally missed and landed. You know, on your head."

He's silent for a heartbeat. Maybe I'm not supposed to tell him about a traumatic event if he doesn't remember it. Maybe I was supposed to make up some crap that wouldn't sound too scary.

"Can I sit up?" he asks.

The other two cowboys just shrug. *Awesome, great support,*

guys. Then again it's not like either of them would expect much assistance. They're the type who don't believe in crying and think whiskey is the cure to just about anything. They'd never drink on the job, but that's about the only place they draw the line.

"Um, I don't know," I say, honestly. Is he allowed to sit up or should I force him to lie in the dirt until we know the extent of his injuries? I turn to Bailey. "Can you go grab Dr. Phillips from the spa?"

She narrows her eyes. "He's a cosmetic dentist. I really don't think now is the time for an emergency tooth-whitening procedure."

I wave my hand around. "Oh, no, not that one. The other one. Dr. Franks or whatever."

"Dr. Franc. He's an acupuncturist. I don't think Landon's in need of stress relief. . . ."

"Seriously, Bailey, just go to the spa and grab the first person you see with 'Dr.' on their name tag, please? Our options are a little limited."

"Okay, okay," she mutters, putting her hands up in a surrender pose. I watch as she jogs across the arena and then slips between two iron railings.

"And you two. Go find Marshall," I say. The barn boss must know what to do in case of an accident, right?

But once they're all gone, I'm alone with Landon and more uncertain than ever.

"Can I *please* sit up? I think my ears are full of dirt," Landon grumbles.

I glance back toward the spa, wondering how long it will be before Bailey returns. Landon *does* look a little ridiculous sprawled out in the dirt. "Uh, I guess," I say. "But don't stand yet. We need to wait for the doctor."

He reaches for my arm and I can't help but assist him, until he's sitting up and oddly . . . leaning on me. I guess he forgot about our fight last night, or maybe his head is pounding so hard he just doesn't care.

We sit there for a second while he gains his bearings, and then he frowns, rubbing his temple. "I feel like I got kicked in the head by Twister."

"Uh, except they got rid of Twister, like, a year ago."

He laughs and then grimaces. "I saw him yesterday," he says. "Out in the west field with the heifers."

I open my mouth to argue, because there's *no way* he saw a bull that's been gone for almost a year, and the heifers aren't even in that field right now, but then realize it's stupid. Who cares about a bull? He probably just rattled some screws loose, and he'll remember soon.

"You're really cute when you're worried," he says, wincing again.

What the? Is he so focused on playing me he'll do it even over a major head injury? I don't know what to say to him, so I just snap my mouth shut and grit my teeth, looking forward to moving away from him once he's been taken care of.

"Oh good, she's coming back already," I say as I spot a little white golf cart approaching the side of the arena, Bailey riding shotgun beside a guy in a silver button-down shirt and baby-blue tie.

We wait as Bailey jumps out, followed by the guy I hope is a doctor, despite his lack of white coat or stethoscope. The man kneels in front of Landon, and I get to my feet, standing next to Bailey.

"Bailey tells me you took a spill," he says. "I'm going to check your pupils for dilation, okay?"

Before Landon can react, the man shines a bright light directly into Landon's eye, causing him to blink rapidly before pulling back and rubbing his eyes.

Without saying anything, the doctor runs one of his hands into Landon's thick blond hair, as if to check for bumps. When he pulls his hand back, Landon's hair is sticking up on one side. "Any dizziness?"

"A little."

"That's normal. If it persists or gets worse, then you should be worried. Headache?"

"Pounding," Landon says, rubbing at his temple.

"Also normal."

Marshall ambles over then, not looking at all in a hurry. He stops next to me just as the doctor stands. "If he starts breathing unevenly, becomes confused and disoriented, or slurs his speech, take him to the hospital. Otherwise it appears to be a standard concussion. Keep him off the horse for a few days, because you don't want a second concussion on top of this one—that can get serious."

I nod. A standard concussion. Right. "He didn't remember what happened," I say.

"Eh," Marshall says, unimpressed. "I got thrown from a stud ten years ago. Still don't remember untacking him or turning him out afterward, but I'm told I did. Landon's a tough dude."

And I swear Landon actually smiles at the praise.

The doctor narrows his eyes. "Right, uh, a little memory loss is common. Some get it back, some don't. It's our mind's way of coping. Don't stress it."

I nod. Right. Okay, then.

"Someone needs to check on him throughout tonight just to be sure he's still feeling okay. Wake him up every hour or so, ask him a couple of mundane questions to be sure his condition hasn't changed."

"Gotcha. I can handle that," I say.

The doctor nods, as if satisfied, and then dusts his hands off. "All right then. You should be fine."

And then the doctor is gone, crossing the dirt.

I turn to Bailey. "Who was that?"

She cringes, her nose wrinkling up.

"No seriously," I whisper to her, just out of Landon's earshot. "I have never seen that guy before."

"Technically he's some kind of nurse."

"I told you to get a doctor!" I whisper-shout, no longer sure it matters, since Landon is so out of it.

"He practically is one!" Bailey says, throwing her hands up. "He does the Botox."

"Bailey!"

"What? I figured he had some kind of training. I mean they let the man stab people in the face with a needle."

I'm chewing on my lip so hard it starts to hurt.

"He seemed like he knew what he was talking about," she says, softer now. "And Marshall's not worried and the dude has probably been bucked off a hundred horses. We watch Landon for symptoms. If he doesn't get worse, he's probably fine. I'll find Dr. Franc later and confirm with him, okay?"

Landon, still sitting near our feet, clears his throat. "So . . . can I get up now? I think I'm sitting on a rock."

I crouch down beside him. "Um, okay, yeah. Let's get you up and to your cabin. You need ice and aspirin and then we can decide if you should hit up the ER."

"No ER," he says adamantly. But I don't miss the way his eyes flick up to Marshall. "I really just want to lie down for a while."

I try not to roll my eyes, wondering if that's really it or if he wants to impress his hardened boss. I mean, going to the ER is so not something cowboys do around here, and even I know it. Upper management would support it, of course, but around the barn it's like a code of honor that you take your licks and keep on kicking. And if it's really just a normal concussion anyway, maybe that's okay for once.

He accepts my hand and that of Marshall as he climbs awkwardly to his feet, swaying. Marshall and I steady him, until he's standing upright. I don't realize I've been holding my breath until a heartbeat later, when I exhale, long and slow. Maybe we're out of the woods.

"You're so good to me," he mumbles, wrapping his arm more tightly around my shoulder and leaning in to kiss my temple. I shoot a panicked look at Bailey.

"What the heck?" she mouths.

"I don't know," I mouth back. His brain is obviously scrambled if he thinks I'm okay with him being all lovey-dovey after last night's blowout.

We escort him down the pathways, Bailey leading the way to cabin 10, a row behind our own. "I'm that way," he says, pointing to a small cluster of cabins across the yellowing lawn. "Cabin six," he says.

"No, you're not," I say. "That was last year."

"I know where I'm staying," he says, leaning the other way, pulling me with him.

"Whoa, whoa, whoa," I say, barely keeping him on his feet. Does this count as disoriented, like that Botox dude said? Or is it the totally normal part of memory loss? "We, uh, moved your stuff this morning. There was, uh, a rat infestation in your original cabin."

I don't know what's up with him, but I'm not about to let him drag me across the ranch when his cabin is a dozen yards away. Not to mention, Grant Porter, one of the oldest ranch hands, is living in cabin 6 this year, and he's grouchy as all get-out. He'd be ticked if we strolled into his cabin just to prove a point to a concussed teenager.

We stumble through his cabin door and I lower him, with considerable effort, onto the couch, dropping him the final few inches. "Owww," he says, leaning back into the armrest. "You owe me one of your shoulder rubs now," he mumbles.

Yeah, right! That is so twelve months ago.

"You be sure to check in with me later and let me know how he's doing," Marshall says as he heads to the door. I guess I knew not to expect much nursing. He's not exactly the type.

"Have you really landed on your head as hard as he did?" I ask, looking up at my boss.

"Sure." He snorts. "He'll bounce back."

I nod. "Yeah, okay. Thanks."

"Yep. And like I said, touch base with me later. I've gotta call in the feed orders."

I watch him go before walking back over to where Landon is sprawled across the couch.

He squints up at me. "I think I hurt my eyes because your hair looks weird. Like a shimmery rainbow."

Instinctively, I dart a hand up to my hair to see if it's sticking up or jacked all over or something, but my ponytail feels normal.

"He's being totally weird," Bailey whispers as we back away from him.

I follow her to the entry, and we stop. "He just landed on his head at twenty miles an hour. He's lucky the steer didn't step on him."

"Hon," he calls.

Bailey crosses her arms and shoots him a glare. "Why does he keep calling you pet names?"

"How should I know?" I whisper-shout. "He thought Twister was still alive, and that he was in the same cabin as last summer!"

"Ew, I'm having total flashbacks," she says, grimacing.

"Huh?" I ask, rubbing my temples, like *I'm* the one who fell off a speeding horse.

"Of last . . ." Her eyes fly open and she gasps. "Ohmygod, ohmygod," she says, shoving me. "Go ask him what year it is."

"What? No! Why?" I don't like the look on her face. The one of total glee that spells trouble in every way.

"This is totally like a movie or something! Like *The Vow*!"

"What?" I ask. "This is not a movie!"

"Then go ask him and prove me wrong! He totally has amnesia! He thinks this is last year and you're together and that's why he keeps playing touch tag!"

My eyes flare wider and I glance back and forth between her and him, to where he's got an arm slung over his eyes.

"He probably just forgot about the bull being culled and he *wishes* we were together, so he's taking this opportunity to become a groper."

"But he thought he lived in cabin six, like he did last summer."

My mouth goes dry. "That doesn't mean anything."

"Prove it," she says, staring me down. "Go ask him what the date is."

"That's such a random question!"

"Then ask him how old he is! If he says eighteen, he's fine, and I'm wrong." Her grin tells me she expects to be right.

I glare at her. "Fine." I stomp across the room, then poke him in the arm.

"Ouch," he says.

"We have to ask you some questions, to, like, make sure you're okay," I say, cringing at how insipid I sound. "That's what Dr. . . . I mean that's what that guy said. To be sure you weren't, like, confused or something."

"All right." He pulls his arm off his face, squinting up at me.

"Where are you right now?" I ask.

"Serenity Ranch. I didn't hit my head *that hard*."

"I know, this is just a test. Next question. Um, how old are you?"

"Seventeen," he says.

Behind me, Bailey shrieks.

CHAPTER EIGHT

Outside Landon's cabin, Bailey paces so fast she looks like she might explode out of her skin. Her adorable leather flats are kicking up a mini-dustbowl as she chatters on. "So he thinks he's seventeen, which means he thinks it's actually *last* summer and you two are still together, and *oh my God.*"

The last words she practically shouts and I cringe. *"Shhh!"* I say, glancing over my shoulder and back into the cabin. "He's brain damaged, not deaf!"

She lowers her voice, leaning in closer, her body quivering with excitement. "You don't get it. Now you can totally screw him."

"Ohmygod, Bailey!" I say, grabbing her shoulders and shaking her lightly. "I'm not going to have sex with him!"

"Not screw him." She laughs in a way that makes me feel dumb, and then pulls my hands off of her shoulders. "Screw *with* him. This is perfect!" She's glowing, bouncing, totally over-joyed that my ex-boyfriend got hit upside the head. Naturally.

I run a hand over my face, failing to follow her line of thinking. "And how, exactly, is his brain getting scrambled a good thing?"

"He thinks you're still together, so just . . . go along with it."

I drop my hand and shoot her an incredulous look, but she's too busy beaming with pride to notice. "Go along with it," I repeat.

"Yes. Let him believe it. Mack, just think about it," she says, her voice serious now. "I saw you fall apart last year." Her expression softens. "I did your hair that morning and I helped you find that god-awful T-shirt, and I was there when you walked in. I saw how crushed you were when you caught him kissing Nata-lie, and you know you didn't deserve it."

"Yeah, but I still don't see what you want me to do."

"Go along with the little romance that seems to still exist in his head, but this time manipulate him. We'll do some research, figure out everything he loves and hates, and you'll be his per-fect girl. He'll fall head over heels for you. Then, when you get tired of the game, *bam!*" I jerk back when she slams her fist into her palm.

My jaw drops. It's . . . totally shady. And maybe a tiny, teeny bit tempting. For once, the player would become the played, and he'd know what it's like. He listened as I told him I loved him, and he kissed me back, and that whole time he wanted Natalie. He dropped me in a humiliating, earth-shattering, confidence-shaking kind of way.

Her words ring in my ears.

"I couldn't do that," I say, but it's a weak protest at best. I *could* do that. He hurt me so much that the urge to do it right back is overwhelming.

"Think of it like community service—he'll probably do what he did to you to a dozen girls. He'll break their hearts. You could make him realize how much it sucks to be hurt by the person you love, thus saving a bazillion hearts from breaking." She nods, totally convinced that this qualifies as charity work. "And, I mean, you get revenge to boot."

"But I can't," I say again.

"You *can* and you *will*," she says, her eyes boring into mine. "It's not like you have to drag it out all summer or anything. Just a few weeks, until you've had your fill of pulling his strings, then you dump him."

"A few weeks," I say, letting the idea settle in. "But what if everything goes fine for a week or two and then he just . . . remembers everything?"

"Contingency plan, Mack. While you're fake dating him, we can screw around with him. Play some pranks to liven things up. No matter what, you win."

I chew on my lip.

"Seriously, you're way too hung up on him. This will be good for you, cleanse your palate. It's one of those what-goes-around-comes-around things, or whatever metaphor should probably apply here," she says, waving her hand in a vaguely circular manner.

I swallow. "So . . . I pretend we're together, like really? Because that means I gotta do it all." I frown. "I mean, he's kinda touchy-feely, you know? I'm going to have to kiss him. Probably make out with him."

She gives me the Look. "Well, play a *little* hard to get," she says, like she can't trust me. "He seems into that."

"Okay," I find myself saying, realizing she'd convinced me three minutes ago. All of this was really just a ruse, because how could I resist the idea of breaking the heart of the guy who'd crushed mine?

"Really?" She grabs my hand and squeezes it in hers. "This is going to be so totally epic!"

"Yeah. Let's do it."

CHAPTER NINE

When my cell phone beeps at one a.m., I slide out of bed, still fully clothed in navy-blue sweats, turned down at the waist, and a faded WSU T-shirt, rubbing my eyes as I creep out of my bedroom door for the third time tonight. Bailey tried to get me to wear something sexier to bed, going as far as offering me her silk "shorts" (do they count as shorts if my butt literally hangs out of them?) and matching cream tank top, but I refused. I don't care that Landon will see me eight or nine times before the night is through. If I'm gonna lose this much sleep, I have to at least be comfortable.

I mean, the first time it seemed kind of fun, slinking around the ranch at night, but now I just want to go to bed. But *noooo,* I'm out here making sure Landon's not bleeding in the head or something.

I click on a flashlight as I slip my feet into worn-out slippers, pushing through the screen door and holding it so that it doesn't slap shut and wake up Bailey. At least one of us should get decent sleep.

I walk the paths, enjoying the silence of the ranch at this time of night. Even the rowdiest of the guests have retired to their private cabins. A few of the cabins, perched high atop the hill, still glow with light. But down here, with the workers who will all be getting up early to muck stalls and trim lawns and serve breakfast, it's dead silent, save the occasional hum of the crickets, a song that won't die until dawn.

I swing the beam around in front of me, following it toward the back pathways leading to Landon's cabin. I walk through the shadows between cabins 8 and 9, until I'm standing on his porch.

I rest my hand on the doorknob, lost somewhere between anticipation and annoyance, before pushing it in, and then I step into the relative darkness of what is his home for the next couple of months. It's always such a surreal thought that the three of us, all teenagers, live on our own for the summer.

I wonder how it will feel to be truly independent. When this summer is over and Bailey and I go away to college, at opposite ends of the state, I hope it's not the last time we ever room together. I hope we finish our degrees and then find each other again, room together in a house or apartment somewhere awesome.

I click the flashlight off as I enter his cabin, navigating via the faint yellow light from a nearby lamp. Even though this is my third trip to his place tonight, I move slowly, paranoid I'm going to trip on a sneaker or something. Just as I'm about to step into his bedroom, something nearby beeps, and I turn to see his phone on the side table, lit up.

Frowning, I walk over and read *low battery*. I'm about to turn back to his room when something clicks.

The date. My heart twists for a second, until I realize the year isn't present, just the month and day. Whew.

Clearly Bailey and I need to spend some time thinking through all the ways Landon could uncover our ploy. I guess it's good that none of us brings a computer to the ranch and there aren't really any calendars hanging around the cabins or the stables.

His bedroom door is open, so I turn back to the task at hand and creep in, feeling like an intruder.

A few days ago we'd hardly spoken in months, and now here I am in his cabin in the middle of the night. The snide comment I made to him about the roller coaster doesn't seem so out of place now.

I step through the door and let my eyes adjust to the darkness until I can see the outline of his body underneath the sheets. At some point he'd kicked off the blankets—probably because it's too hot to use them—and stripped off his shirt. The sheets wrap around him, dipping lower near his belly button.

My mouth goes dry and I swallow, glancing around nervously like someone will catch me staring.

Bad Mackenzie, I think, but still I take one more moment to appreciate the view before walking over to his bed and poking him—hard—with the flashlight.

Without opening his eyes, he reaches over and grabs my wrist, his fingers encircling it in a tight grip. I freeze, the flashlight still in my hand. "You know this would be easier if you just stayed," he says, eyes still closed.

Stayed? No way.

"For you or me?" I ask, feigning flippancy. Hahaha, he wants me to stay over. When he's half-dressed and it's the middle of the night and we're alone. That's hilarious. So totally hilarious. I'm laughing. On the inside.

"You," he says, and it comes out as a breathy whisper. I know it must be because he's not totally awake, that he's groggy right now, but I feel light-headed, off-kilter. "Climb in," he says, and my heart rate spikes all over again. *Climb into his bed?* "Set the alarm. If I slap it off, I'm coherent and you don't have to move. If I don't, I'm brain-dead so you should poke me with that flashlight again."

The air must have been sucked out of the room. Maybe if he had a roommate, or some kind of reason for him to keep his hands off me, but he doesn't. Most of the workers' cabins are really small, and people get to bunk alone. Bailey and I scored one of the bigger ones since we volunteered to room together.

"Glad to see the fall hasn't affected your game," I say, hoping he can't hear the way my heart has galloped to life in my chest.

"I won't touch you, I promise," he grumbles into his pillow. "I can't even think straight with this headache."

I slide my phone out of my pocket and hit the button on the side, then blink against the bright light to see the time. Businesslike. That's what I should go for right now. "Do you want some more Tylenol? It's been four hours."

"Yes," he says, holding out his hand.

"Okay, be right back." I step away quickly and stride to his kitchen, feeling like I can breathe again once we're farther apart. Holy heck, I forgot how irresistible he is. No, wait, maybe I didn't forget that. Maybe that's why I've been stuck on him so long.

Maybe that's the whole reason I'm standing in the middle of his freaking cabin at two a.m.

I shake two pills out of the bottle and grab a glass of water, then return to his bed. He's sitting up, so the sheet covers his lap but none of his upper body, and I thrust the water at him so fast it sloshes over the edge and drips onto his sheets. He raises a brow, but his gaze is kind of lazy, and he's clearly not alert.

"Uh, here," I add.

He accepts the pills and pops them into his mouth, then downs half the glass of water before thunking it on the nightstand and falling back into bed. He turns onto his side, so that I can see the contour of his back and shoulder muscles.

He's killing me and he doesn't even know it.

"I set the alarm for three," he says. "You staying?"

Am I staying? Why does he act like it's no big deal?

"Uh, yeah," I say, after a heartbeat too long. "On the couch."

"Suit yourself." He closes his eyes again.

I spin on my heel and stalk to the couch, vanquishing the image of his half-naked body as I click the bedroom door shut. In the living room, I plop down on the creaky old sofa. People like him—people that use girls—shouldn't be allowed to look that good. It's distracting. It makes it hard to concentrate on keeping him at arm's length.

I roll my eyes at my own stupidity and lie back on the couch.

It's going to be a hot summer.

CHAPTER TEN

At an ungodly hour a few days later, I'm standing behind the desk in the spa, worrying my lip between my teeth as I stare at the front door, waiting for Landon's broad shoulders to darken the doorway.

"You know, the point of this lip gloss is to make your lips shiny and kissably soft, and you're kind of ruining the effect," Bailey says, leaning in for the third time with a red tube in hand.

I sigh and pucker my lips, accepting the extra layer of strawberry gloss, even though the sweet scent is now making me a little nauseous. "I know, I know." As I rub my lips together, she picks up a glass bottle shaped like an apple and spritzes Forbidden Fruit, an "enticing, citrus-scented perfume," all over my chest. It's saturating my skin now, but I don't feel all that enticing.

"Enough with the perfume!" I say, coughing and waving the space around us.

"I'm just trying to give you a very subtle Natalie vibe," Bailey says, frowning.

I sneeze in response.

Bailey's eyes wander over my hair and makeup and clothes. She's totally into this whole quasi-makeover thing. "I mean, not to be horribly blunt, but he dumped you for her. So the thing is, making you a little more like her will appeal to him. In his eyes, you'll be the perfect package, and the more he's into you, the more you can mess with him."

"Somehow I doubt she showers in perfume," I say. "And besides, they broke up eventually too."

"Well, sure, but it's not just the perfume. The lip gloss and the curled hair and all that stuff work in unison. He's going to think you're the hottest girl he's ever seen."

I roll my eyes. "I pity the world if you ever turn to criminal activities."

"I know, I'm totally a mastermind, right?" She beams and drops the bottle into the basket of cosmetics. "Anyway, stand still. Your curls need more hair spray."

I step away. "Take it easy on the product, okay? This isn't *Pretty Woman*. And I didn't look like Natalie last year either, but I managed to keep his attention for a few months. I can do it again."

Bailey doesn't catch my annoyance. She's too busy returning the hair spray to the crate of products she's got stashed under the desk, the one smashed between all the towels we've folded during our tenure.

"I know, I know," she says, picking up a bottle of green nail polish. "And that's enough time for us to manipulate his feelings. If we can't get him to fall in love, at least you get to prank him for a few weeks."

"Exactly."

Bailey loaned me a pair of khakis like the ones I wore last summer when I helped out around the spa, but I refused her vanilla polo. Instead I'm wearing one I took home last September and accidently washed in a bunch of bleach, resulting in a kind of cool tie-dye effect. I'd never be allowed to wear it if the spa was actually open.

I tuck my polo into my khakis, then try to straighten it out just right so it will look more like Bailey's. Trim and presentable. "So, do you think if I look in the mirror and say his name five times, he'll appear behind me, breathing down my neck?"

Bailey's eyebrows furrow, then she reaches out and touches my forehead, like I've gone crazy.

"It's from *Candyman*," I say, leaning away from her outstretched palm. "It was a joke."

"Suuuure."

"It is! If you had watched it with me, you'd know that."

"Mm-hmm . . ." Her voice trails off as she digs through the basket of products.

I watch her, wondering if somewhere in that basket is the magic key to winning Landon over. If there's really a way to transform me into a girl he wouldn't dump at the end of the summer. "What if he doesn't show up? What if he got his memory back after a couple of good nights' sleep and this doesn't work? I've hardly even seen him since he's been stuck on the couch. Mr. Ramsey won't let him ride for a few more days."

"That's the *point* of this," she says. "We have to test his memory loss, and his loyalty. If he *truly* thinks you're together, he should do this stuff for the sake of the relationship. And then it's all up from there. Bigger and better pranks every time."

"I know—"

I'm interrupted by the front door rattling. I glance up and there's Landon, in a shoulder-hugging, worn-out T-shirt, the one he let me wear last summer. I swallow, remembering his tanned skin in the moonlight, the way his shirt had smelled as I pulled it over my head.

He got under my skin so easily and then never looked back, and the thought of it is enough to fire me up. "Well, here goes nothing." I walk to him, smiling as I step aside and push the door wide enough for him to enter. "Come on in," I say, glancing past him to where the sun is kissing the rolling mountaintops.

Revenge is a dish best served early, before the rest of the place wakes up. Bailey and I need the spa to ourselves if we want full control over Landon. He and I are due out in the stables in an hour, but that leaves us plenty of time for what is coming next.

"Hey, babe," he says, swooping in for a kiss.

I stand paralyzed for a second, then dodge his kiss and turn it into one of those horrible, lips-smearing-across-my-cheek-slash-hug things, the sort that belongs in romantic comedies with the bumbling guy who plans to go for a kiss and then chickens out and changes it to a hug. I'm going to need one of those stupid towels to wipe off my cheek. I hope Landon likes the taste of the blush Bailey has dusted on my cheeks.

"Lip gloss," I say lamely, then clear my throat. "I, uh, just put on lip gloss, so no kissing."

Ugh, maybe I really *am* becoming Natalie. Wait, that's probably mean. She's not actually all that artificial, just really gorgeous. It's easy to assume she spends a bazillion dollars on makeup and somehow that makes her really concerned about the wear and tear of her lip gloss.

The thing is, I can't just leap right into the kissing zone, not with him. If I kiss him today, we'll be making out tomorrow, and then what? I *barely* made it through the last summer of temptation.

Arm's length, arm's length, arm's length, I chant in my head.

"Huh," he says in response, his eyes narrowing. I didn't wear lip gloss last year. Or blush. And I didn't curl my patriotic hair.

"Um, anyway!" I say, brightening. "So we asked you to come here this morning because Bailey and I are focusing on adding more, um, guy-friendly spa treatments."

"Guy-friendly spa treatments?" he repeats, an eyebrow quirked. Landon is not a guy who would ever, *ever* set foot in a spa on his own volition. He'd volunteer to help dig a ditch or rescue a kitten from a tree, not offer to help us with this. I'm pretty sure his head was still spinning when Bailey requested he meet us early this morning, because he agreed way too easily.

"Yeah, see, Mr. Ramsey promised me I could have an extra day off if I increase the foot traffic of our male patrons, and we *really* need your help," Bailey says. If I wasn't in on the ploy, I would have believed her myself. She's so good at lying she could be a politician. "You *do* want me to have an extra day off, right? It's like a sweatshop in this place. I'm working so many hours. . . ."

I glare at her. Now she's totally overdoing it. Mr. Ramsey is a pretty fair boss, even if he is a little bit regimented about it all.

"I don't see why you can't just practice on each other," he says, glancing between us.

"We don't know what guys like!" Bailey says, blinking innocently. "Some guests might be more open-minded, but I need to appeal to strong, masculine guys such as yourself."

Holy smokes. Even memory loss wasn't enough to make him this dumb.

"Please?" I ask, realizing I had to dive in before she messed this up for me. "It won't take long. We just need to test some products and get your reaction. Then you wash it all off and head to the stables, and Bailey can do trials on real customers with the stuff you liked."

I step forward, touching the bare, smooth skin of his arm, imploring him with my eyes, and for a second I forget what it is I'm asking, where I'm at, what I want other than to stand there under the heat of his gaze.

"All right," he says, slowly, drawing out the words, not breaking our eye contact.

"Great!" Bailey says. She pulls on his sleeve, and my hand slips off his arm as he steps away.

I get angry with myself and replace the image of his intense look with another one—the one he gave Natalie in the cafeteria at school, just before he leaned in to kiss her. When he pulled back and she whispered something to him, his lips curled up in that way I thought was meant only for me.

No, I'm not going to fall for some stupid look. *He* is going to be under *my* spell.

But first . . . a test.

I follow Bailey and Landon down the hall, to one of the

rooms near the back, the one painted a beautiful, calming blue. In the corner, one of the spa's six water features bubbles, and the edges of the room are lined with stone accents that give the whole place a sort of Roman feel. The only window is draped in billowing gauzy white curtains, so that the sunrise makes the room feel warm and tranquil.

We picked this room because it's one of two with no mirrors.

"Okay, so lie on that table, and then Mack and I will get the products," Bailey says, standing in the hall and gesturing into the room. "You don't have to take your shirt off, but throw on one of those smocks so we don't get your clothes all . . ." Her voice trails off and she smirks, just out of his view. "Mucky."

Landon raises a brow but remains silent.

Does he really trust me that much? Had he really liked me enough to do this by this point *last year*? Because that's where he is, in his mind. We've been dating for two weeks.

I push away my questions and follow Bailey to the back storage closet as Landon steps into the treatment room and the door clicks shut.

"Okay, so how evil do we want to go?" Bailey asks.

Her words echo in my ears as I remember how *I* felt last year. How I gushed about him. How I took such care in dressing that morning, getting to school late because I had to look perfect, picturing myself walking arm in arm with him down the hallways.

Last summer roars through my head like a freight train, one scene after another, culminating in that moment at school when two matching teardrops trailed down my cheeks.

And the jerk simply walked away when he saw it.

"Category five hurricane," I say, burying the hurt.

She claps. "I knew you'd embrace this."

I grin, relief and anticipation and only the tiniest bit of guilt swirling through me. Guilt that is so easy to tamp down.

"Yeah. I'm embracing it. All the way."

Bailey grins. "Awesome. Now go grab the food dye."

CHAPTER ELEVEN

Two hours later, I'm sitting on Zoey, watching as Landon rolls the final barrel into place, then tips it upright. He twists it a few times, so the base digs into the dirt, and then turns to me.

He still hasn't realized his face is covered in blue dots, which nicely complement his tanned skin and dark brown eyes. They turned out better than I could've imagined. Bailey is a total genius, and I hope she never turns her evil ways on me. Every time Landon looks at me, oblivious, I smirk a little and then force a blank expression, because at some point he's gotta wonder why I keep smiling like some buffoon.

"All right, it's all you," he calls out, walking over to the railing. His back to me, he climbs up the pipes, his western button-up straining across his shoulders.

I wait until he's seated—so close to where Bailey and I had sat and discussed IEDs—and then I turn Zoey so my back is to the arena. We're in the chute, a wide area meant to be the entry and exit point for galloping horses. Zoey tenses, something I can feel even through the saddle, as her nostrils flare and she snorts. This is the part I love most. That last second before she explodes on my cue. I may not be pro rodeo material, but there's something pretty epic about controlling an animal of this size.

It's ten a.m., but I'm already sweating in my jeans. My *plain* jeans, the ones Bailey made me buy to impress the Trenton brothers. I'm trying to go back to dressing more like I did last year, so that Landon doesn't figure out how much time has actually passed. And last year, I would've worn these jeans.

I double-check the strap on my helmet, then gather the reins tightly in my hand, taking a deep breath. No matter how many times I do this, I never quite let go of the nerves.

A breath later, I give Zoey all the guidance she needs—a slight pull on one rein, telling her to turn. As she spins, I lean forward so as not to be left behind, and then we're off.

Her hooves pound into the sand as she finds grip, and the wind almost instantly whistles in my ears as we careen toward the first barrel. I sit back as we approach, pulling hard on the right rein and leaning in as she skids around it, and then we're off again, to the second barrel directly across the arena.

She's coming up too fast and wide, so I lean back a little earlier, guiding her around the barrel, and then we're racing toward the third one. To the one next to where Landon sits.

Despite the breakneck speeds and the concentration it takes, I still feel the weight of his gaze as I reach the final barrel. I sit deep in the saddle as Zoey skids, her hooves sliding as she rounds the barrel, and then we're past it, facing the chute again, and she's digging in, flinging dirt behind us as she finds purchase and we're off. I kick hard and vaguely register Landon's deep, loud whistle as we bring it home.

Seconds later I'm standing in my stirrups, leaning back and bringing Zoey to a skidding stop before I lean down and pat her neck. She dances underneath me, amped up by her favorite event.

I turn her and lope across the dirt, to where Landon is sitting. I slow to a walk, using my leg to guide her up against the railing, closer to him.

With me in the saddle and Landon perched on the iron railings, we're almost eye to eye. He tips his cowboy hat back, wiping his brow with the sleeve of his shirt. I frown as I realize the blue dots are already fading, wiping away with the sweat of the day.

"What's with the look? That was a fantastic run," he says.

"Huh?" I blink. "Oh, yeah, I mean, I guess."

"Seriously," he says, practically glowing behind the fading blue dots. "I don't know how you've improved so quickly. It must've been in the sixteens. You were running nineteens last week when we used the clocks."

"What? I wasn't running . . ." Oh, crap. Last year. I was slower then, not quite comfortable enough to push the horse. So to him I went from cautious to gangbusters in a few days. If I'm not careful, I'm going to screw up this whole charade over something as silly as barrel racing.

"Oh, uh, yeah. What can I say? I came here to 'chew bubble gum and kick ass . . . and I'm all out of bubble gum.'"

He tips his head to the side. "That's from *They Live*. An

underrated classic, if ever there was one. I didn't know you liked horror movies."

I almost snort, because we've already established our mutual respect of horror movies. At least I've distracted him from my sudden and drastic improvement in barrel running. "Yeah, definitely."

"Cool. Me too." He holds out his hand so we can bump fists. I knock his, then pick up the rein again. It's completely bizarre to be enjoying an everyday conversation with him. To act like we're friends, not enemies.

"Thanks. That's probably it for the day on barrels, then. End on a high note, or whatever." To be honest I just want to quit because now I'm not sure how to act—do the same thing I just did, or go back to being slow, like he expected me to be? Force the swing wide around the big blue plastic barrels? Knock one down completely?

He nods and slides off the railing, dropping to the dirt. Even on foot, he's tall. Close. He rests his hand on the toe of my boot, and I swear I can feel the heat of it through the thick leather. He seems comfortable, casual, while I'm so hyperaware of his every single touch.

"I'll go grab Storm and we can walk her out on the trails. Give Zoey a break from arena work." He starts to turn away, heading toward the far gates.

"You can't," I say, and he stops. "Remember?"

He levels a look at me. "It's only one day early and I'll take it easy. I doubt falling off at a walk is going to do much."

"Yeah, okay," I say, slowly, not sure if it's a good idea. He took a serious hit to the head. He probably should stay off the freaking horse, but I don't protest. Because I kind of like the idea of hitting the open, dusty trail with him. We did it so much last summer.

"Meet me at the gate in five minutes," he says.

I nod and watch as he slips through the railing and then jogs across the dusty drive, disappearing into the shadowed entry of the barn.

I turn Zoey and walk lazily across the dirt-clouded ring, lengthening the reins so she can stretch her neck. At the gate, I use my right leg to signal a side-step, and she moves to the left, close enough that I can flip open the horseshoe latch and swing the gate wide.

Just as I'm riding through the opening, my cell rings, startling me from my relaxed stupor. I unbutton the little pocket at the front of my western shirt and slide the phone out.

Mom Calling flashes across the screen. I tap and put the phone to my ear.

"Hello?"

"Mackenzie?" Mom says. Like she's not sure who will answer, as if she doesn't recognize my voice or something.

"Yep. What's up, Mom?"

"Just checking on you," she says. "You're so far away, you know?"

I smile. My mom's a stay-at-home mom, and my sister moved out of the house a couple of years ago, so whenever I leave for the summer, Mom never seems to know what to do with herself. After the first few weeks on the ranch, she gets used to it. "I know, Mom. It's just for the summer."

"But you're only back a few days before WSU."

I blink, realizing she's right. I mean, I knew it all along, but hearing it like that reminds me that I won't be *home* much over the next four years. From the ranch to WSU, and then possibly back again. If they'll have me for another summer. "Yeah. It'll be good though. And you can always visit."

I watch as Landon appears at the exit to the barn, leading Storm toward me. The horse is different today. Relaxed and ready for an easy ride.

"Yeah. Anyway," my mom says, "I'm not calling to whine. You got some paperwork from WSU and I wasn't sure if I should open it or forward it to you."

I look at Landon again as he crosses the drive. He can't hear me talking to my mom about college paperwork. I wasn't doing college paperwork last year, because I hadn't applied yet. Neither had he. Did he even know he'd already graduated? Was he going to college too? Maybe me not telling him of his memory loss would have bigger effects, like the part where he forgets to go to college.

No, wait. After I dump him, I'll tell him the truth, because I want him to know *why* I'm dumping him. Want him to know that the pain he's feeling is his own fault.

There's rustling in the background and I realize my mom must be actually holding the envelope in her hands. "Why don't you open it and then call me later and let me know if it's anything I need to worry about?"

"Okay," she says, and I swear she sounds a little gleeful that she gets to open my mail. "Sure."

"Anyway, I gotta get going," I say, feeling a little guilty. "I just finished riding, and—"

"You wore a helmet, right?"

No matter how far apart we are, I always know where she stands and how much she loves me. Unlike how things are with a certain someone. "Yeah. Always. But I still gotta walk her out, so can you call me later?"

"Sure, honey. Love you."

I nod. "Love you too, Mom. Tell Dad I said hi."

Landon's next to me now, putting the reins over Storm's neck. He gives me a sympathetic look, one of those Moms—can't-live-with-them-can't-live-without-them sort of things.

"Will do," she says.

"Bye." I lock the screen, and then slide the phone into my pocket.

"The call is coming from *inside the house!*" Landon says in a mocking, singsong voice as he crosses the reins over his horse's withers.

"That's not how it works," I say, as I twirl a few long strands of Zoey's mane in my fingers.

He slides his foot into the stirrup and swings onto Storm's back, and once situated, picks up the reins. "Not how what works?"

"Quoting movies. It's gotta be subtle, like something someone would actually say. So that way, if you haven't seen the movie, you don't even notice the quote."

"You have *rules* for quoting movies," he says, more of a statement then a question.

"Duh. Anyone can randomly spout quotes. Horror movies, Shakespeare, anything. The game is working it into everyday conversation without getting caught. And as far as I'm concerned, horror movies are the only ones worth quoting."

It's not really something I did, a year ago. I guess that's how we didn't realize we both loved horror movies. Silly that we watched so many movies neither of us actually liked.

"You're serious," he says, a smile tugging at his lips.

"Yep. I do it to Bailey all the time. She hardly ever notices."

"Well, okay then. I guess I just got a little too excited at the realization I wasn't going to be stuck watching chick flicks with you all summer."

"Definitely not," I say.

"Awesome," he says. Then he clicks his tongue and an instant later, we're walking toward the trail head, past a big, dried-out shrub. Our horses' shoes make little clicking noises whenever they kick rocks, trails of dust rising in their wake. Ahead, a magpie sings, then takes flight in a flash of black and white.

"I seriously needed a break from that arena," he says. "I swear even my eyeballs have dirt in them."

"Mm-hmm," I say, already a little lost in thought. Because I'm still not sure how this is all going to go, how I can go back to talking casually with him.

"Summer has a way of feeling longer here, doesn't it?" He pulls up a bit, and Storm tosses his head in protest as I sidle up beside him. Our knees bump as our horses go two-wide on the trail.

"I think it's the heat," I say, lamely.

"It's nice though, right? To wake up every day and know it'll be just like the last."

I narrow my eyes and play with the reins in my hands, two tiny strips of leather that manage to control a thousand-pound horse. Not so different from the feeling of control—or lack thereof—I have over my feelings for him.

"You don't find it . . ." My voice trails off because I'm not sure what word I'm searching for. "Monotonous?"

"What? Waking up and riding every day? Enjoying the out-doors . . . and being with you? No. Not at all."

All at once, I'm blasted with a strange mix of déjà vu and anger.

We've had this conversation before. He might be genuine about how much he likes this place, but he's lying about how much he likes *me*. If he thought I was really so great, he wouldn't have picked Natalie.

"I kinda doubt I have much to do with it," I mumble, but it's loud enough for him to hear.

"I'll admit, being with you makes the summer seem shorter, not longer," he says, grinning. I catch myself smiling back. Dang he's irresistible when he wants to be. "But maybe that's just me."

"No, I know exactly what you mean."

Landon reaches out, playfully pushing my shoulder. "Okay, smart aleck. I get it. I'm being dumb."

"You are not!" I say, suddenly indignant. "I was serious. I get what you mean. Summer here exists outside reality. I think it's because every day feels exactly the same, so it's like the days last forever. You know, like how it must feel in prison."

He snorts under his breath and picks up his reins, which are far longer than mine, the loose end dangling down to his horse's knees. He takes the end and gently flicks them toward my leg. "Exactly. Well, maybe it doesn't feel like prison, though. But here, at the ranch, real life doesn't exist."

I nod. Real life. It definitely exists. And if I forget it for too long, I'll be in big trouble. I'll forget that this is all make-believe and I'll fall for him all over again, like some lovesick dog who doesn't know better.

Screw that.

"Yeah, anyway," I say, ready for a change in subject. "Are you looking forward to the rodeo next weekend?"

He nods. "Yeah. Wish there was some real competition, but it should still be fun."

"Definitely. Although I'm not exactly stoked about pole-bending. . . ."

"You impressed me on the barrels today though. Have you been practicing after I go to bed every night?"

I grin. "Something like that."

"Someday we should convince Mr. Ramsey to have a real rodeo at the end of the year. Invite some tough competition. Make it a big event."

"Why do you want a real competition?" I finally respond, "So you can blow them all away with your superior steer-wrestling skills?"

"Hey, that was a one-time affair," he says, flicking me gently with the reins again. Is he flirting? Wait, of course he's flirting. I'm his girlfriend. "I own that event."

"Uh-huh," I say, egging him on.

"You say that like you don't believe me!"

"Oh, no, I *totally* believe you," I say. "Mm-hmm. Mr. Steer-Wrestling King, riding alongside me just like the common folk."

He reaches out to poke me in the ribs. "I don't know, I think you're the impressive one, shaving entire seconds off your barrels time practically overnight."

"I know, inspired, right?" I say, hoping he can't see the under-current of nervousness I get every time he points out the incon-sistency.

"Yeah, totally," he says, and then his expression changes, along with the tone of his voice. " 'I am your number one fan.' "

"Misery," I say. "You're not going to break my legs and stick me in a remote cabin now, are you?"

"Dang, I thought that one would be too subtle for you." He grins. "But hey, I *do* have a cabin. . . ."

"You have to catch me first!" I dig my heels into Zoey and she jumps forward.

He's still gathering his reins as I bolt away, and Zoey grunts as she lengthens her neck, elongating her stride and sprinting toward the rolling peak in front of us. Then I remember he's not supposed to gallop, not supposed to risk another head injury so soon after the first, and I start to pull the reins, sitting back in my saddle. But then I hear the sounds behind me and know he's forgotten too—or doesn't care—so I lean forward again, urging her on.

The wind whistles through my ears again, and all I can hear is that and my own heartbeat . . . plus the hooves pounding behind me. I don't have to see him to know he's picking up speed, but the trail narrows just ahead, so there's no way for him to avoid the dust kicked up by Zoey's hooves.

I push Zoey faster and faster . . . and faster.

The desert landscape blurs into a mess of brown and sage green, and Zoey's ears flatten as she pushes into her top speed. I finally stand in the stirrups, tugging back on the reins. She resists for several strides, taking the bit in her teeth before finally tossing her head and slowing her gait, just as Landon approaches and pulls up.

In that instant, we're grinning at one another, the kind of wide-eyed beaming that can only be genuine. And I'm transported back to when I so innocently believed that everything was real. Before I realized that he had way more going on than what he let me see.

But at least, in this one euphoric moment, I actually know what he's thinking.

CHAPTER TWELVE

I'm standing next to Bailey, staring at a pile of mashed potatoes, my lips screwed up to the side. It looks like . . . glue. Kinda grayish and goopy and completely unappealing. " 'Soylent Green is people!' " I mutter.

"Are you quoting one of your weird movies again?" Bailey asks from beside me.

"It's not weird. *Soylent Green* is a classic."

"That doesn't make it cool," Bailey says, watching as big glops of mashed potatoes fall off the spoon and back into the vat. "Ew."

"Yeah. Exactly." I drop the big metal spoon back into the tray, and it makes a *plop* noise. Super appetizing.

We slide our trays farther along the buffet, to where the fried chicken sits, and Bailey grabs the tongs, putting a piece on each of our paper plates. Next up is the corn on the cob, which glistens with butter, and then a biscuit. If I didn't spend every day working so hard, I'd probably gain twenty pounds every summer.

Bailey pokes at a pile of green beans, then snarls her lip up in disgust and tosses the spoon back into the bin. "I still think they serve us last night's leftovers for lunch," she says.

"Except it was brisket last night. Chicken was two nights ago."

"Even worse," she says. We grab bottled water, then gather up our trays and cross the little lunchroom, the place reserved only for the workers. It's the original dining room, from when the guests used to dine side by side with the ranch hands.

"Hi, Mr. Ramsey," Bailey says as we walk past where he's sitting with the two assistant managers—one specifically assigned to the golf course and the other to hospitality. They're all dressed in pressed button-down shirts, little gold tags pinned to their chests. I'd be surprised that they're in the staff lunchroom at all, except they've got papers scattered all over the table, so it looks suspiciously like a meeting.

Bailey pauses. "Did Tricia tell you one of the washing machines in the spa is broken?"

He picks up the leather portfolio, snapping it open and scanning down the page. "Repairman will be here between two and four. Be sure the bill is given to Patty in the office."

"Will do."

I muster a little wave as I follow Bailey past their table, and we find seats as far away from the managers as possible. I plunk down on an old chair that has probably been around since the days the ranch held biweekly cattle drives.

"I'm starving," Bailey says.

"Did you fold a thousand towels again? Because *I'm* starving, but I actually mucked stalls."

"Yeah, yeah, I don't deserve to be hungry," she says, waving her hand at me as she bites into a biscuit. "I get it, I get it."

"I'm so not saying that. But you should seriously join me in the stables sometime. I think you'd gain a whole new appreciation for the work I do every day, and maybe even let me take the shower first for once."

"No way, *you* are supposed to join me in the spa. But your stupid blue hair isn't washing out," she says, tipping her head to the side and studying my ponytail.

"I know," I say, reaching up and tucking it farther underneath my Serenity Ranch ball cap. "I thought it would be more temporary than this. I guess I should have used less dye." I screw my lips up to the side. "I just got the *best* prank idea."

Bailey brightens, then claps her hands together. "Oooh, spill!"

"Hey, guys," a voice interrupts.

Adam's standing next to our table, wearing dirty jeans and a T-shirt with the Serenity logo on the chest, his floppy brown hair falling into his eyes.

"Oh, hey," I say. "What's up?"

"Just grabbing lunch," he says.

"Come sit with us," Bailey says. "Plenty of room."

"Nah, I'm in a bit of a rush."

"Are you sure? Because the two-day-old chicken is *delicious,*" Bailey says.

He chuckles. "No, I'm actually on my way out to the green," he says, glancing at his watch. "One of the big lights is down and apparently some VIP guys are expecting to do some night golf."

"Fascinating," Bailey says, like she actually means it. She turns closer to him, propping her elbow up on the back of the chair and leaning toward him. "Your job must be *super* interesting," she says.

He glances over at me, like he can't figure out if she's being sincere or she's messing with him. I don't think the poor guy has any idea that what she's doing is supposed to be flirtation.

"Fascinating," I say, once he's out of earshot. *"Your job must just be sooooo interesting."* I twirl my hair around my finger and bat my eyes over and over again.

"Shut up. Flattery usually works," she says.

"I can see why. It's so *genuine.*"

"I'm serious! Guys love their egos stroked. I don't know what his deal is."

"Maybe you found the one guy in the world immune to your charms."

"Not happening," she says with vehemence. "He'll be eating out of my hand by the end of the summer."

"Mm-hmm," I say, nodding my head exaggeratedly.

"Why are we talking about *my* love life? We have serious scheming to do when it comes to *yours.* Tell me about this idea you have."

I grin. "It requires a little more thought, but . . . do you think you can get more of this blue dye?" I ask, pointing to my hair.

Her eyes light up. "Are we going to dye his hair while he's sleeping? Or put it in his shampoo somehow?"

I shake my head. "Nope. Think bigger. Get some red too."

"I'm *dying* of suspense!" she says. "Just spill already!"

"Sorry, I'm keeping this one close to the chest for a little longer. But it's genius. Totally genius. He'll rue the day. Rue it, I tell you."

"You suck." Bailey pouts.

I laugh, enjoying that I have the upper hand for the first time in, well, ever. "You'll find out tonight," I say. "I'm going to need some help."

"Okay fine," she says, watching Adam as he crosses the room. He gives us a little wave, and she waves back before looking at me again.

"All will be revealed. Just be at the cabin by ten and we'll sneak out together."

"Yeah, yeah, be all mysterious then." She downs the rest of her water, then turns and tosses the bottle toward the nearest recycling can. It bounces across the floor, echoing loudly, but she doesn't move to pick it up. Instead she just turns back to me. "We should actually stay up late tonight and preplan a ton of pranks, you know? How many do you think we'll need?"

I shrug. "I figure I'll just prank him until I am sure he's in love with me.

"The biggest prank of all is that I'm not really dating him. So if he doesn't get his memory back, we'll go to the big dance and I can dump him afterward," I say. "That's, what, six weeks from now?"

"Yeah. Makes sense," she says. She looks over her shoulder as a guy walks by, stooping down to pick up her discarded bottle. She waves at the random dude and mouths, *Thank you.* Man, what it must be like to know the world revolves around you. She turns back to me, smiling. "Okay, so I just got my own genius idea," she says.

"Oh, great. I love your genius ideas."

She laughs. "You shut up. You really do love them. Without me your life would be Boringtown, USA."

"Yeah, yeah. Genius idea. Get to it."

"We should totally go on a double date. I'll get a date for the Fourth of July. We can all watch fireworks together."

"Sure." I stand, shoving my chair back and gathering what remains of my lunch. "Landon and I are teaching lessons again this afternoon, so I gotta jet. See you at the cabin later?"

"Yep." She nods, making no move. She has exactly an hour for lunch and she'll use every last minute.

"'K, bye," I say, walking away, stepping through the door and out into the sunshine.

I shouldn't be looking forward to seeing him so much.

CHAPTER THIRTEEN

"Where are we going, exactly?" Bailey asks, walking beside me on the cement pathways, a paper bag with little twine handles swinging in her hand. I know it contains the promised blue and red dye, and it's almost impossible to resist snatching up the bag to be sure she has enough.

But Bailey is nothing if not dependable. She's got what I need.

"The stables," I say, glancing around to see if anyone is watching us. "And seriously, do your shoes have to be that loud?"

"They're flip-flops!" she says, sticking her foot out and shaking it around. "There's no way to walk in them without the flip and the flop!"

I roll my eyes. "I swear if those dumb sparkly things get us caught . . ."

"If I had known we were going to be sneaking around in

broad view, I may have planned accordingly. But someone was being all secretive and didn't tell me what was going on."

"Sorry," I say, glancing back at Logan's cabin one more time. There's a lamp on but no movement. "I had to do some Googling to be sure this isn't, like, inhumane."

"Hair dye?"

"Yeah." I take in the silent, shadowed stables. "Or, well, fur dye."

There's a beat of silence before she reacts. "Oh my God, you're a *genius!*" Bailey hollers.

"Shhhhh!"

She lowers her voice, leaning in. "We're totally dying the spots on his horse, aren't we?"

"Yes. I'm thinking we can dilute it down a little so it won't last as long, but he'll have to ride like this in the rodeo."

"I take back everything I've ever said about your lack of scheming skills. I love this."

I bow, accepting her praise. "Good. Because it's going to take a while, so I need your help."

"At your service," she says, saluting me.

"Mr. Ramsey is going to hate it, but Landon is one of the most exciting guys to watch in the rodeo. No way is he going to boot him."

Once at the barn, we slide the door open just enough to slip in, and then pause to allow our eyes to adjust to the darkness inside. I flip on just one switch so that the lights at the far side of the stables click on. Lucky for me, Storm's stall is at that end, near the wash rack.

"So that stall there has an extra door to the paddocks. I figure you can peek out periodically and see if anyone is coming," I say, taking the bag from Bailey. "If all is quiet, come down and help me in ten minutes."

"Aye, aye, captain."

I walk down the aisle and slip into Storm's stall, then bring him out and clip him into the wash rack. I step back, studying the piebald pattern of his spots. Lots of white to cover. Hopefully it works better than the blue dots on Landon's face.

I work in silence for a while, enjoying the companionship of Storm and the promise of Landon's reaction when he sees what I've done to his most prized possession. I know a prank like this could drive him away, and ruin my grandiose plan of dumping him, but I don't know for sure that his memory loss is permanent. These pranks are the only way to ensure that I get *some* form of revenge, even if it's not the crushing blow I'm hoping for.

Ten minutes later, Bailey joins me, working the red into a spot on Storm's shoulder.

"Okay, so we should brainstorm what we can do to make sure he falls for you," Bailey says.

I squeeze some more blue dye into the white spot behind Storm's withers. "Definitely. Any ideas?"

"Well, I spent a while on his Facebook page today," Bailey says. "He doesn't have it set to private."

"And?"

"I wrote down a few things we can use to make you seem like his perfect girl."

I crouch down, running some blue dye down Storm's front leg. "Like what?"

"He's super into the Seahawks," she says. Storm sighs deeply, clearly enjoying the massage-in of this dye. "He likes a few of their fan pages and talks about Wilson Russell—"

"Russell Wilson," I correct.

Bailey leans over so that she can see me past Storm's body and eyeballs me. "Since when do you like football?"

I shrug. "My dad talks about that guy all the time. Plus Landon has that Seahawks shirt he wears to school."

"Oh, so you've been paying attention to him all year," Bailey teases. "So just regurgitate whatever your dad has said about Russell Wilson, and Landon will be all ears."

"Done. What—" I stop abruptly. "Did you just hear something?"

"No, why?"

"Shhh!" I freeze, leaning toward the aisle. And the unmistakable sound of boots hitting the cement floor.

Bailey's eyes flare wider.

I take in a few ragged breaths of air, trying to steady my heart, and then lean slowly out of the wash rack to see who is coming.

Marshall is heading straight toward us.

I jerk back into the wash rack and close my eyes for a second to keep from freaking out. I think my heart is trying to climb out of my throat.

"It's my boss!" I hiss.

"What do we do?" Bailey whispers.

I shrug and mouth, *I don't know.*

The footsteps grow louder, and then he stops just shy of the rack. A callused, tanned hand reaches around the corner for the light switch that controls the fluorescent fixture above Storm's head.

The rack goes dark, and his footsteps retreat. I blow out a silent breath.

And then Storm stomps a foot, his steel shoe clacking on the cement.

Marshall's footsteps return and the light flicks back on, and I'm crouched there, blinking up at him.

Crap. I am so busted.

His eyes sweep over the horse, taking in the red and blue spots we've completed so far. He glances at Bailey first, then his gaze settles on me.

Please do not fire me. The panic rises. I stand, meeting Marshall's gaze.

"I take it Landon doesn't know about this?" Marshall asks, hooking his thumbs into his belt loops. He's nothing like the trio of managers Bailey and I encountered earlier today. His jeans and boots are, like, a million years old, and his button-down lacks any semblance of the crisp shirts worn by Mr. Ramsey and his minions.

Yet the hardened cowboy is no less intimidating.

"Uh, no," I say. "I thought it could be, uh, you know, a surprise." I add an arm flourish.

Marshall's eyes sweep over the horse again, and then he leans over and spits.

My heart beats so loudly I think he must hear it.

"Fine by me," Marshall drawls, and hope surges in my gut. "But if Mr. Ramsey has a beef with this and it causes trouble for the barn, we'll be having another talk," he says. And when he meets my eyes for a final time, his meaning is clear: we can have our fun, but not if it brings him trouble.

Relief swirls through me. "Of course," I say.

"Okay, then," he replies, spinning on his heel and ambling off.

"Holy crap, I thought we were toast," Bailey says as soon as he's out of earshot.

I laugh. "Me too."

"You're right about one thing." She picks up the red dye again.

"What?"

"The barn is a way cooler place to work. My boss would've cited the rule book and written me up or something."

I squeeze some blue dye into my hand. "Nah, we kinda run in our own circle. Mr. Ramsey tries to pretend he knows all about horses, but he doesn't. He's pretty hands-off."

"He runs a much tighter ship in the spa," she says. "He pops in every other day, and every time I think I might pee my pants. Do you think he checks up on the maids and, like, bounces quarters off the sheets?"

I snort, not because the idea is ridiculous, but because I could actually see him doing just that. "Anyway . . . back to the task at hand. Anything else you think I can use on Landon?"

"He seems to like pickled things."

"Huh?" I say, frowning. "I mean I've seen him eat pickles before, but I don't see how that helps me."

"No, I mean pickled asparagus and pickled jalapeños and stuff. He uploaded a photo of this giant jar of them and it was almost empty."

"Who the heck uploads pictures of pickle jars?"

"Your *boyfriend,* apparently. You must be the luckiest girl on the planet."

I snicker. "Okay. So I talk football and eat pickles. Got it."

"Yeah. But okay, now here's where it gets super weird."

"Pickles wasn't it?"

"No. Anyway, he and his buddy got into this huge debate a few weeks back. We're talking like a hundred and twenty-two comments back and forth."

"About what?"

I can't see her expression, but I *know* she's grinning from ear to ear, just by the tone in her voice. "Well, he has very strong opinions about Chuck Norris."

I burst out laughing so hard, Storm startles, tossing his head up. I slap a hand over my mouth. "Chuck Norris?"

"Yeah. Whether he'd beat Batman in a fistfight."

"And? Which side did he fall on?"

"Landon feels strongly that Batman is just a buff guy with gadgets and that Chuck has more experience in hand-to-hand combat."

"He seriously argued about this."

"Yes. The one thing I realized, as I was skimming his page, is that he very much enjoys debate."

"You mean he likes arguing," I say. "I noticed that last year, but I never really dug in my heels. Like I thought he'd get annoyed with me, so I was always like, *Oh, you're totally right. I agree.* Except it killed me to do that."

She bursts out laughing. "Since when do you admit someone else is right?"

"I know!"

"I can't believe you did that. Do you remember when I told you you'd argue whether the sky was blue? And you were like, *Well today it's not really that blue anyway, so . . .*"

I lean forward to where Bailey is crouched and push her just hard enough that she kinda falls back on her butt and laughs. "You know I'm right," she says. "So maybe you've met your match. I mean, it's not an argument in his mind—he likes to actually *debate*. He kept using all these Chuck Norris photos and links to YouTube videos and quotes from some fan pages and everything. Supporting his argument. So I think you should pick a few hot-button things and enjoy a little healthy debate with him."

"You think if I disagree with him, he's more likely to fall for me."

"Yes. He's really competitive about it. The Chuck Norris debate didn't end until his friend conceded."

"Huh," I say, stepping back to admire Landon's treasured horse, which is starting to resemble our lovely American flag.

"Yeah," Bailey says, coming around the horse to stand beside me, grinning when she sees the results. "So I suggest you develop some very strong opinions on a variety of subjects."

CHAPTER FOURTEEN

When I walk into the barn the next morning, whistling Landon's beloved national anthem under my breath, my step falters. Six people, Landon among them, are standing near the bulletin board, leaning over one another and peering at a sheet of blue paper. They don't hear—or choose to ignore—the sound of my steps on the concrete as I approach.

Being short has its advantages, and I slip in between them, pushing my way to the board to see what has their attention.

Summer Barn Schedule

This must be why Marshall came down to the barn last night. I scan over the lists, seeing my name highlighted under **Barrels** and **Pole Bending** for the upcoming rodeo, and then again under . . . **Cattle Drive.**

I don't get any further into the schedule before I turn to

Landon, who's stepped away from the crowd and is waiting for me, leaning against the wall.

"We're going on the cattle drive again," I say, walking over and high-fiving him.

"Again?" he asks, quirking a brow.

My heart spasms in my chest. "Uh, I mean, we're going," I say, cursing myself for the slip. I stare right at Landon, trying to remember if blinking too much or not at all is the telltale sign of a lie. "The *again* was because . . . you know, we're doing the rodeo and the drive. So we're on two lists."

"Ohh. Yeah. Cool."

Instantly, images of him and me on the cattle drive—the one he doesn't remember—barrel through my mind. Riding side by side down long, dusty trails, falling behind to push the straggling cattle back up to the herd. Swimming at the end of a long, hot day. Sleeping on the open ground, staring up at the stars. Me, a little bit sunburned but completely, blissfully happy.

All of that shattered a few days later.

There has to be a way to mess with him on the cattle drive. I'll have hours and hours to spend with him. It's a good thing I have weeks to figure it out. It's one of the last events of the summer, right before the dance.

"Awesome," I say.

"Anyway, I need to pick up a couple of things in town tonight. Do you want to go out to dinner?"

I blink. "Dinner? Like a date?"

Ugh. Dumb, dumb, dumb. I'm so constantly reminding myself that we aren't really dating, that I just totally screwed up.

"Yeah, you know, that thing guys do with their girlfriend? They sit down at these little tables, pick up menus . . ."

"I know, sorry. I'm being silly. It's just . . ." My mind scrambles. "It's been, like, two weeks since I left the ranch. I guess I forgot a whole world existed out there."

"Then let me show you. We can head out around six?"

I nod. "Sounds great."

The two of us walk down the long cement aisle a ways, and my anticipation grows as we get closer to Landon's horse. I click my tongue at a few of the horses as I pass, causing them to swivel their ears at me, and then we reach the end, where the wheelbarrows are kept. "I'll take Musa's side if you take Storm's side," I say.

He nods, tossing pitchforks into each wheelbarrow, and then we go to the first stalls. Landon is unlatching the stall door, so I stand in silence behind him, waiting. Finally, the latch pops and he slides the door open, simultaneously looking up.

Silence.

I wish I wasn't standing behind him, because I can't see his expression. But then his shoulders move, the tiniest tremble at first, until they shake, and then he leans over and bursts out laughing, a deep throaty laugh that is as sexy as anything I've ever heard.

Storm steps forward, as if confused by Landon's reaction, and when his head swings out the door, I can't help it. I laugh too.

His forelock, which had been the only white part on his mane, is varying strands of blue and red, and Bailey added polka dots to the blaze running down his face. The rest of him is an alternating patchwork of red and blue, and in the end he looks like some psychotic clown's horse.

Landon turns to me, and I can't help but grin back at him when his gaze meets mine. His eyes sweep over my hair, then back at Storm, taking in the identical colors. "Nice work," he says, wiping a tear from his eye. "Epic."

Part of me is annoyed that he loves it, but the more dominating part just grins back at him. And then I curtsy in a ridiculously over-the-top way, pretending I'm some Southern belle. "Why, thank you, kind sir."

He shakes his head and turns back to the stall. "Oh man, I'm going to be the best-dressed dude at the rodeo," he says.

I smirk and finally slide my own stall door open, to where a gray Arab stands chewing on breakfast. I push my wheelbarrow into the stall, then reach over and flip on the radio mounted on the wall at this end of the barn. Country music—the only thing allowed in the barns—streams out of the old speakers.

We work in silence for a few minutes, scooping out the used bedding and tossing it into the wheelbarrows with muffled thuds.

"How's your mom doing, anyway?" he finally calls out.

"My mom?" I ask. She got in a car accident last fall and had to have surgery on her knees, but if he doesn't remember the last year . . .

The silence in the barn is louder than the radio, but then he clears his throat. "Yeah, didn't you say one of her good friends moved away or something?"

That did happen last summer. My mom's friend from childhood—the one who had bought the house next door a dozen years ago just so they could stay BFFs forever—moved to the East Coast for a job. I almost forgot about it. "Oh, yeah, I mean, she's fine. The people who moved into our neighbor's house are cool, I guess. She's planning a DC trip in December."

"Good, good."

"Mm-hmm. What about your sisters?"

"Just as hellacious as ever," he says, and across the aisle, through the metal bars on the stall front, I see his grin. "Jenny is fifteen already," he says.

Sixteen, I think.

"She brought this date home the other day and I think I terrified him."

Landon's dad bailed on the family when he was a kid, and he's got that whole man-of-the-house thing going on. He probably totally loves harassing his sisters and their dates.

"Somebody's gotta do it," I say, pulling some of the cleaner shavings toward the middle of the stall.

"That's what I said."

I set my pitchfork down and dig into my pocket, glancing over a bullet-point list I created this morning based on five minutes of Googling things on my phone. Let's hope the hordes of Internet message board users employ valid arguments.

"So, Bailey and I were talking about 007 this morning," I say as I shove the list back into my pocket.

"Oh?"

"Yeah. See, I think Pierce Brosnan is the best James Bond of all time, but she's all about Daniel Craig," I say.

"You're both wrong," he replies. "Sean Connery is the only Bond. The others are just imitators."

I turn toward the back of the stall to hide my gleeful expression. Man, this is almost too easy.

"No way," I say, turning back to the bedding. "Brosnan embodies the suave, totally unshakable quality required of a true secret agent." I try to sound as if I believe everything I'm saying to the core of my being, but it's hard. I've never even seen the Brosnan versions.

"Connery is the *original*. You have to take into account that his movies were filmed in the sixties, when special effects weren't as great as they are today. He *carried* those films."

Bailey was right about one thing. He's enjoying this, spouting facts and trying to prove his point. It's like I sparked a fire.

"Yeah, but Brosnan took the helm after a six-year hiatus." I pause and dig the paper back out, scanning my eyes over the facts. "And plus, his films are the first of the series to *not* use plotlines from the novels."

"Yeah. They could do that because *GoldenEye* had a big budget. Money to hire good writers, create awesome stunts. But when Sean Connery portrayed the character, the entire movie cost, like, a million dollars or something."

"Yeah, but even Roger Ebert said that Brosnan was the best."

"Brosnan took the helm of a white-hot Hollywood property and carried it for a while. It's not that hard to drive a train when it's already barreling down the tracks."

"Maybe, but they were big shoes to fill," I say. "A lesser actor would've coasted by on his predecessor's interpretation of the character. Brosnan brought wit and charm."

"Connery had an accent. That alone makes him more

charming." Landon pauses, as if he just realized what he said out loud. "Or so I hear."

"Pierce Brosnan is Irish! Connery is Scottish. There's hardly a difference," I say, looking up from my pitchfork. Landon meets my eyes, and I see that fire practically sparking in them. He is *determined.*

"Maybe, but Texas beats Scottish or Irish any day."

"I *suppose,*" I say.

"What? You know girls love a Texan drawl. I mean, you do, obviously."

"But not as much as something European," I say. "It's more exotic."

"How did we go from debating James Bond to accents?"

I toss my pitchfork into the wheelbarrow. "I don't know, but I'm sure you're wrong on all accounts."

"We'll see about that."

Landon pulls open the passenger door, motioning into the truck, and I slide onto the leather bench seat, the material hot on the backs of my bare legs.

He didn't do this for me last year. Didn't take me on a formal date outside of the ranch. I have no idea what that means. Is my scheming actually working?

I force myself to stop analyzing his actions. Instead I fix my skirt as he slams the door, the solid steel clanging hard. It's an ancient Chevy, something from the seventies that Landon supposedly fixed himself, back when he was sixteen. It sat, immobile, in the auto shop at our high school for almost a year. I guess I'm lucky he didn't fix it last winter after our breakup, or he'd wonder how it had miraculously turned into a flawlessly running machine. Man, I'm not sure how I'd explain that one.

Landon slides in beside me, and as he fires up the engine, his eyes sweep up and down my body. "So, you staying all the way over there the whole way into town, or . . . ?"

I roll my eyes and slide over, until I'm sitting in the middle of the big bench seat, our sides touching. He rests his hand on my knee. "That's better. A guy doesn't buy a truck with a bench seat for nothing."

My cheeks flush a little as he puts the truck in gear and we back up, then turn down the long paved drive of the ranch. It was a huge expense, black-topping something this long, but Mr. Ramsey insisted that the guests who arrived in their pricey foreign cars would hate the gravel that existed last year.

Just as we're halfway down the drive, Landon hits the brakes.

"What?" I ask when he comes to a full stop but doesn't speak.

"Was the driveway done up like this when we got here?" he asks, twisting around in his seat.

Oh. "Uh, yeah. I mean, they did it earlier this spring, I guess."

"That's weird," he says, turning back to the front. "I could've sworn it was gravel."

"Nope. Been blacktop the whole time we've been here," I say, avoiding eye contact and trying not to sit too stiffly.

He narrows his eyes and for a second I think he's going to disagree, but then he just releases the brake, and we're gliding toward the road. A minute later, he turns onto the county high-way and picks up speed, until we're barreling down the pavement at sixty, the windows rolled down and the hot, dry desert air whipping my hair in a thousand different directions. He rests his left arm on the windowsill, moving the other from my knee to the wheel.

I watch the rolling hills and dry sage roll past the window as I reach down and flip the radio on. Nothing but static crackles through the speakers, so I punch the dial a few times, and when it still hisses, I smack the top of the dash.

Landon reaches out to bat my hand away, swerving the truck a little in the process.

I make a phone out of my thumb and pinky finger. "Hello, 'I'd like to report a truck driver who's been endangering my life.'"

"*Duel.* And I'm not endangering your life, you're endangering my forty-year-old radio. It's original. Be gentle." He reaches out and spins a knob, and the static gives way to a familiar tune: the one we danced to together last year.

"Ugh, change it," I say.

"No way. I like this song."

I did too, once.

I put my hand back in my lap, and he grabs it, so that our clasped hands rest against my leg. I lean my head back against the sliding glass window behind me and let myself get lost in the song, in the contentedness of being with him on the highway, somewhere between our relationship on the ranch and the reality of home. His hand is warm and callused and way too perfect in mine.

Twenty minutes later, we're pulling in at an Italian restaurant

I've never noticed before, sandwiched between a grocery store and a gas station. The big red awning and pretty scrolling script, proclaiming *Versanos,* beckons us across the lot, and soon he's holding the door open for me again and I step through.

"Hi, two for dinner?" a hostess asks, beaming at us from behind a podium.

"Yes, thank you," Landon says, and I follow him as the hostess leads us to a wraparound booth in the back, where a little candle in a jar flickers. We slide in on either side of the table but end up meeting in the middle. We accept our menus and then silence falls around us.

I don't know how to act right now, on a date like this. Last year we always just hung out, watching movies apparently neither of us even liked and sometimes kissing. Were there rules, expectations, when one went on a formal date? Do we make small talk and end it with a kiss on the porch of my cabin? And how the heck did I get to be eighteen and still so ridiculously anxious about stupid stuff like this?

"I'm looking forward to the cattle drive," he says, after a few minutes.

"I know. It should be *so* fun."

"We're going to be stuck training the guests, you know. Since we're the lesson teachers."

"That's okay. I mean, they kind of slow things down. . . ." I stop myself. I shouldn't know this. "I mean, I'm sure they'll slow us down, but it won't be bad."

"We should sneak out an hour early and just do the drive ourselves," he says.

"I think we'd be fired."

His hand finds my knee under the table, and he rests it there. "True, there's always that."

The waitress walks up then, interrupting the moment. "You guys know what you want?"

I haven't even thought about it, but when I pick up the menu, it's impossible to resist the idea that lodges in my head. "I do," I say.

"Go ahead." Landon nods.

"I'll take the surf and turf," I say, tapping on the menu.

The forty-two–dollar surf and turf. I force my face to remain neutral as Landon searches for the item on the menu. I wait for him to react as he realizes the price.

"Um, actually, that sounds great. Me too."

Him too? This is officially the most expensive date I've ever been on.

"Uh, can I get a strawberry lemonade as well?" I say, smiling sweetly at the waitress.

"You got it." She gathers our menus and then disappears, and there's an awkward pause. I half expect him to call me out on my pricey selection, but he doesn't, he simply sips at the water glass in front of him.

"Can I ask you a question?" I say, a heartbeat later.

"Sure. Shoot."

"What is it you love so much about riding?"

He releases my leg and sets both hands on the table so that he can fiddle with the cloth napkin. It's like I've struck a weird chord, flipped a switch, and he went from happy little Landon to serious Landon.

"You want the real answer or the short answer?"

"Real," I say, wondering why there's a difference.

"My dad left when I was ten."

"Right," I say. I knew this, since long before we talked about his sisters while we were mucking stalls today.

"I idolized him, you know? I thought he was such a *man*. Really tough. He nearly cut his finger off in a chop saw once, and he barely flinched. Just calmly wrapped it up and asked me to go get my mom. I never saw him cry or anything, either. And, well, there's just something about the cowboys that are like that. The way the horses and the cattle and the guests always come first. They're real men, you know?"

He pauses for a long moment, and the silence gets awkward.

"I don't know what to say."

"I'm not done yet. You said you didn't want the short version." There's something a little tense about the way he says it, so I nod, urging him on.

"I feel like I've spent my whole life trying to be there for my sisters because he's gone. Somehow the hole he left is just too big to fill, no matter how hard I try. Yet when I think of the cowboys, it becomes more concrete. Something I can handle."

"Oh," I say.

"That's why I like riding," he says. "Because I don't have to think. I just live by a certain, basic code of honor. Those guys may be rough, but they're men. And sometimes when I'm around them, I think maybe I'm just as good as they are."

There's such a raw, hoarse honesty to his tone I believe everything he's saying, which only makes this all the more confusing. Because a man who wants to desperately prove himself better than his father's legacy doesn't dump a girl like he did with me.

He didn't even freaking dump me! He just started making out with his ex-girlfriend.

"That . . . makes sense," I say, swallowing down the odd bit of emotion that is bubbling up at his confession.

"You think?"

I nod. "Yeah. Can I ask you another question?"

"Sure."

"It's more serious than the last," I warn.

"*More* serious?"

I nod.

"Okay."

"If we were to invent robots that could do everything for us—cooking, cleaning, babysitting, walking our dogs, driving our cars—do you think they'd take over the world and kill us all?"

He half snorts, half laughs, and I find myself grinning at him.

"Well, let's agree on the basics, first. They'd have to have a certain amount of artificial intelligence, right? In order to adjust their behaviors as necessary. Even a perfect assembly line can manufacture defective products, so the robots would need to be able to identify problems and exercise judgment."

"True," I say.

"So we're talking about robots with actual intellect. Eventually they realize what a bunch of screwups human beings are, and they eliminate us. It's inevitable."

"No way," I say, shaking my head vehemently. "They're robots. Even if they did decide to kill us, we're still the superior being. We put a stop to it. Shut them down."

"You're *assuming* we're smarter. We do dumb stuff every

day. Just watch the news for five minutes. You'll find some idiot who decided to gamble at a casino for six hours and he left his kids in the car, or a guy who calls the police because Burger King is out of Whoppers. That *actually happened.* The robots would do a better job of running the world. Easy."

"There might be some idiots out there, but look around. Everything we have was created, was dreamed up by a human being. A robot lacks imagination. Their plan would be predictable. You can't win a war anymore by marching onto a battlefield. It's about smarts, creativity."

"You assume they won't evolve, though. They could easily—" He stops when the waitress walks up, holding two overflowing plates. She sets them in front of us, then sprinkles a little bit of freshly ground pepper on top before smiling and walking away.

Showtime.

"Oh, shoot," I say, frowning at my plate.

"What? Something wrong?" He scans my plate.

"Um, no. I just thought that the surf meant they served the steak on, like, a surfboard," I say, gesturing at my plate and trying desperately to obliterate the urge to grin like a big ol' idiot. He can't possibly be buying this, can he?

"Huh?" he asks, furrowing his brow.

I point at the giant, *expensive* lobster tail on my plate, trying to give him the most puppy-dog, innocent expression I can muster. "I totally hate seafood," I say, frowning. "I'm super sorry, I guess I should have paid more attention to the menu."

He glances at our plates, no doubt calculating the almost hundred-dollar tab between the two of them.

"Not a problem."

And then before I can move, the lobster tail is gliding between our plates, sliding onto his. "I love lobster."

"Oh. Uh, great."

And thirty minutes later, he's proven it.

I might not be hurting his heart just yet, but at least I got to his wallet.

CHAPTER FIFTEEN

I'm stooped over, pulling rocks out of the underside of Zoey's hoof, when someone approaches from behind. The steps are familiar, a casual stroll that can only belong to one person.

"Admiring the view?" I ask, then straighten and turn around, dropping Zoey's foot back to the ground.

"Maybe," Landon says, crossing his arms. "I mean if the opportunity presents itself, you can't fault a guy for checking out—"

"Yeah, yeah," I say, fighting a blush as I wave my hand. "How many in the two o'clock class today?"

"Six."

"All right," I say, tossing the hoof pick into the nearby grooming supply bucket. "Meet you out there?"

"Actually, I just passed the guys in the south wing, and they're pretty short-staffed. Since you're ready to go, do you wanna go help tack up the guest horses? I'll get Storm ready, and then I'll bring them both out for us."

"Oh. Uh, sure. See you in a few," I say, wandering away.

I slip through the gate to the indoor arena. It's too small for our group lessons, but there's two tween girls, seemingly more interested in gossiping than riding, plodding around on fat little gray horses. I wait for them to pass and then exit through the other gate, so I'm now in the opposite wing.

"Roger?" I call out, glancing into the first few stalls.

"Down here," he replies, and I find him in the second-to-last stall, slipping a halter over the head of a bay with a graying muzzle.

"Need a hand tacking up?"

He quirks a brow, and that's when I realize that Landon didn't actually ask if they needed help, which is probably why he sent me instead of doing it himself. First rule of cowboys is they never admit they can't handle a job. "Uh, sure, I guess. Tack the dun at the end."

I nod and set to work, running a quick brush over the mount before tacking him up. I lead the horse out, pausing just long enough to let Roger out in front of me. Seconds later, two other guys emerge from the opposite wing of the barn just as we do, and I suddenly understand Roger's odd look.

They're not short-staffed at all. Three hands is plenty to tack six horses in time for the lesson. Which means Landon is up to something. My heartbeat quickens as I scramble to think of what it could be. But if I could predict Landon's actions, I wouldn't have been so blindsided last September. I have no idea what he's thinking right now.

My radar perks up, and I know, in an instant, that he used

this chance to mess with me. But five minutes isn't possibly long enough to dye Zoey's blaze blue or red, so why'd he want to bring her out for me?

I lead the dun mare over to the far gate, where the guests are standing under the shade of an enormous oak tree, and arrange the reins for the rider before giving her a boost. She's tiny, barely five feet, and I easily help her aboard.

"Go ahead and warm up, and we'll get you going in a minute," I call out to the group as they walk away, paralleling the pipe-rail fencing.

Finally, I turn away and head to the opposite end of the arena, where Landon is standing with Storm and Zoey. Storm's red and blue are practically neon, even from across the ring, and I know I shouldn't have trusted him with my own horse after dyeing his. I can't actually see her, just her chestnut legs, because she's standing behind Storm.

Landon's tossing the reins over Storm's neck as I arrive and round his horse to grab my own.

And then I stop dead in my tracks.

Because Zoey shrank.

I stare at the little chestnut pony with a nearly identical blaze. It's wearing my saddle too. "Oh my God, where did you get this thing?" I ask.

"What do you mean, where did I get it? That's totally your horse."

I giggle. "Uh-uh. Where is Zoey, really?"

"I have no idea what you're talking about."

I turn to him, taking in the smile that he can't quite wipe off his face. "You can't be serious."

"What, you have something against ponies?"

I dart a look at the pony again. "I mean, at least it's not a Shetland. . . ."

He pats me on the back. "That's the spirit."

"But I'm not riding it for a whole lesson," I say. "I'm going to look like a moron."

"Sure you are. You ride that horse for every lesson."

I cross my arms. "Are you sure this thing is even broke?" For all I know, the horse has never been ridden.

He gives me an indignant look. "Of course she's broke."

"You really expect me to believe this is Zoey."

"Absolutely," he says. Then he turns away, trotting toward the group and leaving me standing there with a pony whose back is barely above my belly button. This horse is a good foot shorter than Zoey.

"Hey," I call out, and he stops, turning back to me. "Where's my horse, really?"

His grin widens. "Nowhere you'll find her. So if you want to make these guests real happy with their lesson, I suppose you ought to climb aboard."

I gotta hand it to him. She does kinda resemble Zoey, if Zoey had been hit with a magic shrinking gun. This little trick of his might be more embarrassing than riding a tricolored horse.

"He better be right," I say to the pony. The only sign she's listening is a little flick of her tiny ears. "If you're not broke and I fly off, I'm blaming him."

I toss the reins over her neck and bring her fully into the arena, closing the gate behind me. My best guess is she's a Welsh or maybe a Pony of the Americas or some other little breed. She's lucky I'm barely a hundred pounds. She's plenty big enough to carry me without trouble, but it doesn't mean I won't feel like a big old idiot.

With a deep breath, I climb aboard, waiting to see if Landon even bothered to check the training of my replacement mount. The pony doesn't move, so I nudge it with my ankles and she reluctantly steps out, and soon we're joining the others on the rail.

Landon rides up alongside me, and now I feel utterly ridiculous. I have to crane my neck to peer up at him.

"We look like circus rejects," I say, motioning to my tiny mount and his rainbow gelding.

"I didn't want you to feel left out."

"Naturally," I say.

"We could trade," he offers.

"And give up my stunning pony? Of course not."

"Mackenzie! Landon!" A voice barks out, and my stomach sinks. Mr. Ramsey strides toward us. Landon and I share an *oh crap* look before we turn our mounts toward him and walk over.

"What exactly is . . . this?" He motions to our horses.

"What?" I say dumbly.

His jaw tenses. "Why does this horse match your hair?"

"It was a surprise for the guests," Landon interjects. "They *love* it."

"Seriously!" I say, my mind finally jumping into gear. "Especially the kids. You know how the Fourth of July weekend is our big family weekend. We thought the kids would get a kick out of it, and they've been talking about it all morning."

"Really," he says, his voice flat, disbelieving.

"Yes," Landon and I say in unison.

"And the pony?"

"Zoey threw a shoe," I say. "I didn't want to be late for the lesson and make the guests wait. I don't mind looking a little silly in order to keep them happy."

He narrows his eyes, as if he's pretty sure he can see right through our story, but he doesn't call us out. "Very well. Just see to it that the horse returns to normal after the rodeo. I don't care if you have to shave it."

"Yes, sir," Landon says, and I dart him a look, not surprised he responds to Mr. Ramsey's military authority in the same way I do.

We watch him retreat, disappearing up the path toward the guest registration building, and then we turn back toward our lesson.

"Whew," I say, breathing again. "We're lucky he doesn't realize you can't shave a horse's summer coat. Storm would be bald."

"I know, right? This dye better wash out." Landon laughs, gathering his reins and calling out to the group, "Okay, go ahead and pick up a trot."

Seconds later, I realize I should have taken him up on his offer to trade mounts. I forgot the true bane of any pony owner: the trot. The plucky little thing has tiny little strides but she makes up for it in speed, which results in feeling like I'm riding the top of a jackhammer. I try to post—alternating standing and sitting with each beat of the trot—but it's nearly impossible, and when I blast past the larger, more relaxed horses, I can't miss the couple who glance at me or the ridiculous grin on Landon's face.

He is going to pay for this one.

CHAPTER SIXTEEN

"His name is Ronan," Bailey says as she pulls the tank top over her head. It's still on a hanger, so she's just draping it across her body to see whether it matches her jeans. Because apparently, jeans don't actually match every top.

You learn something new every day.

She yanks the top over her head and sticks it back in the closet.

"And Ronan is . . . ," I say, waiting for her fill in the blank as I take a sip of my soda. I turn back to the belt buckle sitting on the coffee table in front of me, tilting my head to the side to get a better view. When I realized Landon put on a pair of cargo shorts and a T-shirt and left to go to town, I snuck into his cabin and swiped this thing. He won't notice it's gone until tomorrow, when he goes to put on his Wranglers again.

Landon's lucky buckle consists of a man, horseback, roping

a little calf. I'm trying to decide how I can turn this image into something totally mortifying in the next several hours. That's all I've got before he'll realize it's gone. I've gotta creep into his cabin by five a.m. at the latest and return it to his dresser.

"He's a guest. He's staying in cabin twenty-three."

Without looking up from the buckle, I stick out my finger and make a circular motion, as in, *get to the point already.* "And you met him . . ."

"At the concession stand," she says. "I was getting a slushie. He bought it for me."

"Sounds like a keeper," I say, reaching for the little carton of acrylic paints I bought in town this morning.

I have an idea.

"None of them are keepers," she says, pulling the shirt over her head and dropping it on the floor. "I mean, it was totally sweet of him, but I'm not marrying the dude. We're going to college in two months, Mack. Places to see, boys to kiss." She makes a duckface in the mirror. "So anyway, he's taking me off-campus—"

"Do you think that's a good idea?" I say, turning back to my paints. I twist the lid on several different options—white, purple, even gold—and reach for a clean brush.

"Huh?" She stops digging and stares at me as if she just realized I was there. "What are you even doing?"

"Messing with Landon's belt buckle. He wears it to every rodeo." I hold up the buckle, wiggling it around a little before setting it back down. "Anyway. The not-so-good idea: to leave the ranch with a complete stranger," I say. "There's a ton you can do here, and then maybe leave the ranch on your second date."

"Ew, no. He's a guest, and he asked me out for a date in town." She stares into the mirror, holding her hair up off her neck. "What are you even doing to that thing?"

"I'm not sure yet," I say. "And anyway, don't text me constantly or anything. But at least text me in a couple of hours and let me know how it's going, so I know he's not an ax murderer."

"Okay, Mom," she says, rolling her eyes and turning back to the mirror.

I cross my arms. "I'm serious."

"Fine. I'll text you. But once or twice. Anything more and he'll think I'm being rude."

"Deal. And if you forget, I reserve the right to sic Landon on you." Because even though he might be the worst boyfriend in the history of the universe, I believe him when he says he watches out for his two sisters. If I asked him to, he'd probably crash Bailey's dream date just to be sure the guy isn't a creeper.

I blink. When did I decide he was anything more than a royal jerk?

"Ah, Landon. Speaking of . . ."

"There's not a lot to speak of," I interrupt, dipping the paintbrush into the gold paint and brushing it over the front of the calf. The buckle started out gold and silver, but this particular gold is a wee bit more gaudy.

"So that *wasn't* you two heading out on the trails this afternoon?" She grins at me in the mirror, looking like she caught us making out or something.

"You saw us?" I dab a little more glittery paint onto the buckle, until the calf turns into a shimmery unicorn. Awesome.

"I'm surprised, what with your big slushie expedition and all. How'd you find the time?"

"Nice change of subject. And anyway, of course I saw you. You're on horses. And his has giant red and blue spots. Not exactly low pro."

"We were just walking out Zoey again. I practiced poles today. For this weekend's rodeo. I'm supposed to ride in it, in case you forgot." I drop the gold paint and pick up a clean brush, dipping it into the purple.

"I didn't forget. My role is relegated to the ticket booth. Not a lot of practice required."

I hold up the buckle. "What does this look like to you?"

She steps closer. "A guy in a purple dunce cap catching a unicorn?"

I laugh. "Close." Then I dip the brush in some more paint. "Landon is going to go insane when he sees this."

Bailey goes back to the mirror, twisting the top part of her hair and frowning at her reflection. "Anyway, how are things going with him, really? Do you think he's falling for you?"

I dab a little more white onto the belt buckle, elongating a few points until they start to resemble stars in the night sky. Landon is going to look *fabulous* at the rodeo. "Surprisingly, yeah. Our relationship is kind of different this year."

"Yeah, because you're screwing with him, smarty."

"No, I mean, I almost think I'm seeing more of him. Which is weird. I mean, it should be more artificial, right? But last year, in retrospect, it's kinda like we were trying to be this perfect boyfriend-girlfriend, instead of being ourselves. He told me some stuff about his dad that he'd never mentioned before."

She snorts. "So you think this year your relationship is more *real*."

"What's so funny about that?"

"Because you're faking like you're his perfect girl, instead of being yourself! Surely you see the irony."

I freeze. Am I actually being someone else? Or is it actually the opposite? Somehow this version feels more like the real me than last year.

"At least tell me you've used my research." Bailey tips her head to the side as she studies the lavender blouse she just draped over her body.

"Yeah. That tip on debate? Genius. I suddenly must be right about *everything.*"

Bailey laughs, then tosses the halter top she's holding on top of the pile of clothes avalanching off of her bed. "That sounds so . . . unlike you."

"Shut up," I say, tossing a Q-tip at her. I add a little more purple to the buckle, then grab the little vial of gold glitter. "Anyway, the important thing is that Landon's gonna melt down when he sees this."

CHAPTER SEVENTEEN

As the sun rises over the rolling hilltops on the Fourth of July, I shove the last wheelbarrow of soiled horse bedding out the back door of the barn, down the little path, and onto the cement slab. I tip it over and drag it backward, then let it slam down with a clang.

Done.

The sun beaming down makes the dust and any loose strands of blue hair from my ponytail stick to the back of my neck, and my hands are sweating inside my leather gloves. I yank them off and shove them into the back pocket of my jeans, shaking my hands around briefly so they can dry, then I roll the wheelbarrow to the empty storage area at the back of the barn.

The entire ranch is bustling with activity at six a.m., all of it prep work for the rodeo. Every guest suite is booked, and half the town comes to the ranch to watch the rodeo or play in the annual golf tournament. Tonight, ten thousand dollars' worth of fireworks will be detonated. Everyone who lives for miles around will watch the show, as if it's a big billboard for the ranch and the fun you can have if only you pony up the cash to stay here.

Or if only you work here, like me and Bailey and Landon. Despite the fact that we work our butts off all summer, it manages to be the best job in the world. Freedom and adventure, romance and . . . a million things wrapped into one. Today is the most exhausting and fun day of the whole summer.

Once the wheelbarrow is put away, I head out to the driveway, to where a half dozen trailers are parked, two more pulling in just as I round the corner of the barn. The dust kicked up by the tires drifts toward me, rising higher, just like the early-morning sun.

"Mack, can you take her? She goes in stall fourteen, and she's a little too much for me to handle."

I'm surprised to find Adam in the midst of the horses. He's more than a little bit frazzled, the hair under his ball cap sticking out at a million different angles as a horse pulls at the end of her striped red lead rope, her ears swiveling constantly, her nostrils flaring.

"You got it," I say, reaching for the lead. He passes it off, looking instantly relieved as the lead rope leaves his hands. She dances beside me, swinging wide as we head toward the barn entrance.

"Easy," I say, watching her ears move toward the sound of my voice. I slow as we step up onto the concrete, not wanting her to panic in the smaller space, but it's here where she calms, her muscles relaxing as her dancing steps turn into a slow walk.

"Good girl," I say, leaving one hand on the lead as I reach out, sliding my hand down her neck. She leans into me slightly as we continue down the concrete aisle, her horseshoes clip-clopping as we go.

The mare is one of several "loaner" horses that come in the weekend of the rodeo, to ensure we have enough fresh horses to put on a good show. About two-thirds of the rodeo competitors are ranch workers or friends of Mr. Ramsey, but several people from town come in and compete too. But it wouldn't be enough of a show for the guests if we didn't round out the roster ourselves.

I put the mare in an empty stall, one with a bucket of fresh water and clean shavings, and then return to the driveway, where I fetch four other horses, one by one, steadily filling up the empty west wing of the barn. Bailey drifts over as I shove the final stall door shut, the wheels screeching out in protest.

"Don't look now, but Adam is walking toward us," she says under her breath. I glance over, taking in the slight flush in her cheeks.

"Yeah, he's helping with the horses but I get the feeling he doesn't know what he's doing. We're kind of shorthanded this year without Tyler."

"What happened to Tyler?"

"He broke his leg, remember? Anyway . . ." My voice trails off as he approaches.

"Hey, Adam," I say brightly. "You need me to take the little guy?"

"This is one I can handle," he says, stopping in front of us and giving the pony a friendly pat on the shoulder. "He's a wild one, but I got it covered."

If I didn't know better, I'd swear the horse raised one brow, as if to say *yeah, right.*

Adam tucks his thumbs into the belt loops of his jeans, and the way he slings his hands, it tugs at his pants, revealing the edge of his hunter-green boxers. I don't miss that Bailey's eyes dart down to check him out, and then she leans against the wall. "Are you riding today?"

Adam glances over at her like he just noticed she's standing there. "No, not much of a rider. Just helping out at the ticket booth."

"So am I!" she says, her enthusiasm apparent.

"Uh, great," he says. "Looking forward to it."

"Me too," she says. Any guy in a thirty-foot radius is normally pulled in by her flirting. It's as if she's a magnet.

"Anyway," he says, glancing down at his dirty boots. "I gotta get back to work. Catch up with you ladies later," he says as he strolls away, those same work boots thunking on the cement walkways.

"Mmm, mmm, mmm," Bailey says, watching him go. "Blue jeans never looked so good."

"You are insufferable," I say.

"And yet you can't help but love me, right?" She watches him until he disappears around the corner, and then turns to me. "At least he's doing the booth with me. I'll finally get the chance to talk to him for more than two seconds. And then, of course, he'll be smitten by my inner brilliance."

"Your inner brilliance," I say.

"Yeah. I mean for some reason it's not insta-love for him. So I'm going to be all conversational, or whatever, and prove I'm not just beauty, I'm brains too. And then he'll realize we're fated to make out."

I roll my eyes as I walk away, waving to her over my shoulder as I meander down the long concrete aisle and out the back of the barn, wondering if Landon has discovered his belt buckle yet.

I'm walking back to my cabin, planning to grab a water bottle before the crowds arrive and everything on campus goes crazy, when the sound of a slamming door jars me from my stupor.

I turn in the direction of the noise, just in time to see Landon bounding down the sidewalk.

In an instant, the blood drains from my limbs. His sleeves are rolled up to his elbows, and his fists are clenched so hard his lower arms are tight, the muscles well defined. He's on the warpath, his eyes blazing with more fury than I ever thought possible.

This can't be over the belt buckle . . . can it?

"Landon." I stop in the middle of the walkway, watching as he bounds down the sidewalk, a man on a mission. It's like he doesn't see me, just continues toward the stables.

"Landon!" I scurry after him, grabbing his arm and yanking. "Stop!"

He whirls, his eyes on fire. "What!"

The air leaves my lungs. I've never seen him angry at all, let alone this enraged. "I just—" I swallow, looking down at my feet. But as I do so, a dash of rainbow paint and glitter catches my eye. His fists aren't just clenched. He's got something in his grip. I reach forward, to grab the buckle, but he yanks it away.

"I don't have time right now." He goes to shove his way past me, but I don't move.

Instead, I push back with both hands. "Stop."

He hesitates, his chest heaving, his rage coming off him in waves.

"What are you doing?" I ask.

He stares past me, toward the stable, and I wish he would just meet my eyes.

"I told Brooks about my lucky buckle yesterday, and now he's made a mockery of it. It's *ruined*. I'm going to find him and destroy him." He steps around me, continuing his path to the stables, and my heart climbs right into my throat.

It's all fun and games until someone gets hurt. And with his deadly expression, that someone was about to be Brooks, one of the other guys who participate in the roping event.

I race back around, planting myself in front of him. *"Stop!"*

"Mack, I swear to God, you've gotta get out of my way. *Now,*" Landon says, pushing past me once again.

I grab his sleeve and yank. "I mean it. *Stop.*"

"No. Brooks—"

"It wasn't Brooks!" I shout, my voice echoing off the nearby cabins.

His eyes finally meet mine, searching them, as my words register. His expression goes from one of cold fury to bitter disbelief. He's actually disappointed in me. It's there, in his eyes, plain as day. "Tell me it wasn't you. Promise me it wasn't you."

I want to deny it. I want to say someone else covered that entire buckle in rainbow paint, turned it from a cowboy roping a calf into a wizard roping a unicorn, complete with the stars and the moon, but the words die in my throat. His eyes are alight, not just with anger, but something deeper, something darker. Something I've never seen before.

Betrayal. I've destroyed something so much more meaningful than just a silly lucky charm.

I try to swallow around the boulder suddenly lodged in my throat, but it's impossible. "It was . . ." I take in a jagged breath. "It was me."

The words come out on a whisper of air, yet somehow they deflate him. He shakes his head, backing away from me.

"I didn't know it was so important to you," I say, suddenly filled with such overwhelming remorse, my feet feel heavy as I chase after him. "I'm sorry. It was just a joke."

His jaw is clenched so hard I half expect his teeth to crack. The impenetrable Landon is shaken, angry, inside out and backward. But he doesn't speak, just stands there, his chest heaving.

"Why are you so upset?" I ask, stepping closer. Relief swoops through me when he doesn't retreat any farther. Instead, he allows me to touch his arm.

He doesn't answer at first, and I fear I've lost him. But then he rakes in a deep breath, those shoulders going from stiff to drooping.

I slide my hand across his arm, looping my hands behind

him and leaning in, until I'm embracing him, my arms around his waist, leaning against his chest. He doesn't respond immediately, but finally, he lets his arms encircle my shoulders. And we're standing there, in the middle of the workers' cabins, as he shudders, letting go of the rage that has just consumed him.

"It was my dad's," he finally whispers against my ear, too low for anyone else to hear, even if they'd been standing three feet away.

Sorrow and regret swoop through me, so intense I want to flee, go back to my cabin and burrow my head in my pillows.

His father's.

I am a first-class jerk.

"He won it at his last rodeo, before he left us, and I found it in some of his stuff that my mom boxed up," he says, his breath hot on my skin. "I've done every event wearing it."

"Oh God, I'm so sorry," I say, my stomach twisting painfully. "I had no idea."

He doesn't tell me it's okay. He doesn't say he forgives me. Instead, we just stand there, me rubbing his back, listening to the jagged edges of his breathing.

"I'm sure I can get the paint off," I say, but I'm not as sure as I try to sound. I don't know what kind of metal it is, or whether the paint I used could eat away at the finish. I didn't think beyond the decorating.

"It's fine," he says, but his voice has turned hollow, and it's like he's retreating.

I've hurt him.

Deeply.

"Landon, I'm sorry—"

"It's fine." He looks down at the buckle, then whirls away from me, grunting as he throws, with every ounce of strength, and the buckle sails through the air, into the rocks and tumbleweeds. "It's stupid anyway. I shouldn't be hanging on to anything from the loser who left us."

And then he walks away, and I'm left standing there, completely off-kilter.

CHAPTER EIGHTEEN

At any moment it'll be death by rattlesnake bite, because I keep turning over rocks and digging around in crevices. I'm filthy, from head to toe, and my fingers are split and bloody from digging into the weeds.

It takes me nearly an hour to find the buckle.

Cars have been pulling into the grounds for the last twenty minutes, and if I don't hurry, I'm going to miss the opening ceremonies. Mr. Ramsey will kill me. But now I'm so relieved I can't bring myself to care. I clench the buckle in my hand, racing back to the cabin, hope and fear and a thousand things whirling through me.

I have to fix this. I don't know why. I should be gleeful that I hurt him so much. But that tiny triumphant voice in my head is so drowned out by regret that I can't listen to it.

The Landon I saw, vulnerable and raw and hurt, has to go away. I'll give anything to return him to his cocky, comedic, debate-master self. I'm afraid to acknowledge what that even means, how my feelings for him have shifted so abruptly.

I bound into our cabin, slamming the door open and rushing into the bathroom. I grab the first tub of toiletries I find and dump it upside down. Bailey's cosmetics tumble out onto the floor.

And then I see it.

Nail polish remover.

I grab the bottle and rush to the kitchen, yanking a few paper towels off the dispenser and plunking down on the barstool. I put a bunch of nail polish remover on the paper towel, but just before I touch it to the buckle, I pause.

What if I make it worse? What if I ruin it forever and he can't forgive me? The remorse pumping through my veins is terrifying.

I don't want to hurt Landon. Not like this.

Oh God, for some stupid reason I care about him. This is bad. Really, really bad.

I wipe furiously at the buckle, willing the paint to disappear, to reclaim what the buckle used to be. Nothing happens, and I cry out, tears threatening to spill over.

But then the tiniest bit smudges away, revealing the gleaming silver again. And I sniff back the tears, wiping with renewed vigor, as more of the buckle reveals itself. Ten minutes later, when the stupid unicorn and wizard are gone and it's just the silver and gold again, I could faint with relief.

Instead I stand so fast the stool falls to the floor, and then I run from our cabin, leaving a hurricane-size mess behind.

* * *

I find Landon in Storm's stall. He's leaning into the horse but not speaking. I want to rush in, show him I fixed the buckle, but I find myself staring, watching the way his hand rubs lazy circles on Storm's neck. Landon buries his face in the horse's mane, and I watch his shoulders rise and fall.

And now I can't remember why I hated him so much.

"Landon?" I say, unable to play voyeur on this private scene any longer.

He stiffens, knowing I've caught him in a moment I wasn't supposed to see. His shoulders rise and fall a few times, and then steady, and he turns to me, his eyes dry, accusing.

"I'm sorry," I say, holding out the gleaming buckle.

He doesn't meet my eyes. "Is it . . ."

"Fixed. I think. I don't know, I might've ruined the finish."

He runs a thumb over the surface, studying the contours, the contrast of the gold and silver. "Thank you."

"I was the one who wrecked it in the first place."

"You didn't know."

I didn't. Two summers together and I had no idea the buckle belonged to his long-absent father.

"I should've."

The silence stretches on. And then, "No. You couldn't have. I hardly talk about him. I don't even know why I did at the restaurant the other day. It's better to act like he never existed in the first place."

"Why?"

"Because I shouldn't care about the guy who left us behind, let alone his old buckle." He chews on his lip. "Wanting Daddy back is something little kids do. I'm old enough to know better."

I shove the door open wider at that, and step into the stall. He looks up, and his eyes are misty. "Oh, Landon," I say, stepping forward. He finally turns away from Storm and leans into me, wrapping me up so close it's like we're the same person. "Everyone wants their parents in their life. No matter how old they get."

He reaches up, sliding his fingers into my hair, playing with it in a way that feels good, intimate. I close my eyes, and we stand there like that for so long I'm convinced the rodeo could be over, that the entire holiday has come and gone. But then he sighs and pulls away, smiling softly. "Thanks."

"What are girlfriends for?" I say, surprised at the way the words roll off my tongue.

Surprised at the truth in them.

Because that's who I want to be.

His girlfriend.

CHAPTER NINETEEN

I'm sitting atop Zoey in the chute as I listen to the announcer welcoming the crowd. There must be two thousand people filling the stands, another handful of people walking up and down the aisles, selling popcorn and cotton candy. The whole place has a sort of carnival feel to it, people shouting, bulls snorting, the loudspeaker blaring.

The guy on the microphone is welcoming everyone to the greatest show on earth, which I always thought was a thing reserved for circuses. Zoey's ears swivel back and forth as she listens, but she's at ease in the hustle and bustle, alert but happy. She's the sort of horse that will never really retire, just work and work and work until the day she dies.

Kinda like the cowboys around here.

"You ready for this?" Bailey asks. She's standing in front of me, holding the gate.

I nod, one hand on the reins and the other holding on to a flagpole. A barely discernible breeze lifts the edges of the flag.

"Yep. It's my favorite part of the day."

"So, why are you so tense?"

"Long story. I'll tell you later," I say, just as the opening chords of the national anthem play, blasting through the speakers mounted on telephone poles high above the crowds. I have to clear Landon from my head and think of the task at hand. "Let's do this."

I pick up my reins, tighten my grip on the flagpole, and nod at Bailey. She swings the gate open, and I nudge my horse into motion. I pick up an easy lope as I exit the chute.

Soon, I'm paralleling the stands, a thousand people right next to me as I pick up speed. I tighten my grip on the flagpole as the wind pulls at the red, white, and blue, and I feel the flag whipping harder against the air. Two-thirds of the way down the ring, I turn Zoey to the right.

"Whoa," I say under my breath as I near the center of the ring, leaning back and into my saddle. Zoey executes a perfect sliding stop. I turn her so that we face the announcement booth just as the anthem hits its high notes, and the crowd reaches a dull roar.

When the song ends, I spin my horse back the way we came, picking up an easy lope toward the railing. Once there, we head to the chutes at the far end of the arena.

When I exit the chutes and I'm back into the dusty empty driveway, Bailey shrieks. "You were awesome!"

I grin back, her enthusiasm infectious. "Thanks."

"Seriously, that sliding stop was so awesome. No matter

where we are next year, we have to come back just for the rodeo, okay?"

No matter where we are. Bailey's going to UW in the fall, and I'm going to WSU. We'll be six or seven hours apart. The girl who inspires me every day will no longer be my roommate. But only during the year. Not in the summer. I don't care what it takes, we'll be back next year. "Deal."

"Okay, well, I guess I better go work the booth now. My epic romance with Adam is commencing in ten minutes, you know. I'll try to poke my head out when you do your runs, okay? Don't fall off or anything," she says, disappearing into the crowd.

I start to give her a smart-mouthed reply, but a voice stops me. "Hey. You looked great," he says.

I turn to see Landon riding up on Storm, the horse fully equipped for the day—a rope dangles from the horn of the saddle, looped over and over again, and Storm's legs are in red, white, and blue pro boots to protect his bones and tendons. The wraps perfectly match the ridiculously colored spots all over his horse.

"And you look like Uncle Sam threw up all over you," I say before I can stop myself. I'm not sure if I'm allowed to joke right now.

He snorts. "You're just jealous."

"You know it," I say, relieved at his reaction. I take my eyes off the horse and allow them to drift over Landon, searching for some hint of his earlier distress. He's got on those same battered, beaten Justin cowboy boots, the ones he was wearing the day he saluted my hair, before he ever hit his head. He's also got on a familiar pair of jeans, and they're so well worn I want to reach out and touch them. The shirt though, it's new, just like mine. Bright red, with a blue pocket on the front, and a white star stitched in. And in the middle of all that is his gleaming buckle. My eyes linger on it for a minute before meeting his eyes, but he's not the shattered boy of earlier today. Instead his expression is passive, at ease.

"You know what's weird?" He rides up closer, our horses facing opposite directions, our knees bumping against each other. Storm is taller than Zoey, so Landon's looking right down at me, as if from up there, he owns the world.

"What?"

"I swear I've dreamed about this before or something. I got total déjà vu watching you do the flag ceremony."

"Weird," I say, my heart skipping a beat. "It's probably just because you've been to so many rodeos."

"Yeah. Maybe."

I swallow. "So, uh, still no helmet, I see," I say, tapping on the hard plastic surface of my own headwear. It makes a funky *bonk* noise, as if to prove how hard it is.

"Nah," he says, waving his hand. "I mean, I won't bull ride without one, but—"

"You are *not* bull riding," I say, my voice rising an octave.

"Aw," he says. His thick lips curl in an irresistible fashion, and I have the most overwhelming urge to kiss him. "Is someone worried about me?"

"If you bull ride—with or without a helmet—you're gonna end up as a french fry. A human french fry."

"*The Hills Have Eyes*," he says. "I love that movie. And I'm not actually bull riding," he adds, grinning. He reaches out and pokes my arm. "But thanks for the sentiment." His expression is taunting.

"Any time." I reach out and shove his shoulder, retaliation for poking me. But instead of getting me back, he searches the crowd.

"Have you seen my mom around at all?"

My stomach drops. "Your mom?" I squeak.

"Yeah. She's in Leavenworth for the weekend and she was going to swing by and say hello. She usually wears this ridiculous flag shirt and a headband with stars that bounce around on the end of springs. Every Fourth of July, without fail. Seen anyone like that?"

No. No, no, no. "Uh, I don't think so."

"Hmm. I'll go find her. I thought I could introduce you guys."

Crap. He can't introduce us because I've met her before. Last summer, when Landon introduced me as his girlfriend. I forgot that she does a girls-only vacation in Leavenworth every Fourth of July, and it's just over an hour to our west, making it convenient for a drop-in.

And if he introduces me as his girlfriend again, like I've never met her, he's going to know something is off. Everything is going to come crashing down. I'm not even certain how I want the rest of this summer to go; I only know that this game, this relationship, can't end so soon.

I swallow down my panic. "Anyway," I say, turning Zoey away from him, "barrels are up in a bit so I'm going to head to the other arena and go warm up. See you later?"

He nods, his eyes hidden in the shadows thrown by his cowboy hat. I can't help but fear that he'll see my panic, my desperation to get away from him.

I push Zoey into a jog, crossing the lot and heading in the direction of the warm-up ring. Once out of view, I'll find Bailey and we'll figure out how to handle Landon's mom.

CHAPTER TWENTY

Spotted her. Next to the concession stand.

Relief barrels through me as I read Bailey's text message. I slide Zoey's stall door shut and text back, You're a lifesaver.

I've been searching the crowd for two hours—in between my events—and haven't seen her yet. My only solace is the fact that Landon hasn't either, but it's all going to end if I don't get my butt over there before he gets into some deep conversation with her. There are a hundred things she cannot possibly discuss with him—college, his sister's upcoming *seventeenth* birthday, the fact that I'm the same girl he dated last year. . . . Even the tiniest thing could tip him off, lead to questions I don't want to answer.

With Zoey quietly munching on an early dinner, I hustle down the aisle and back out into the sun, scurrying toward the concession stand. I've decided to stay hidden, at least at first. I'll try to eavesdrop on their convo and see how things go. It's always possible they'll talk about something totally harmless. Landon might not even mention me by name. And if he does, there's always the chance his mom doesn't recall meeting me last year, or that she forgot my name.

If I stay out of view, she might not even figure it out.

My phone chirps again.

Hurry. Landon found her.

I pick up a jog, dodging a kid with a red-white-and-blue balloon bouquet and ducking under some tree limbs, my breath growing labored in the hot afternoon sun. Twenty feet shy of the concession stand, I spot her. She's in the same ridiculous shirt and headband as last year. Landon's hugging her, and she's doing that motherly rubbing-his-back-midhug thing. For a second I feel a pang of longing for my own mom. She would totally hug me and buy me lunch and ask if I was too hot and if I've been drinking enough water, if she were here right now.

I shake away the thoughts. *Focus.* I slow, heading to the shady side of the concession stand, and then creep up slowly so they won't see me.

". . . that was a heckuva run," his mom is saying.

"Yeah. It's my personal best," Landon replies, beaming. "Better than the one I did in Monroe last spring."

I cringe, hoping his mom doesn't keep close tabs on his steer-wrestling times. He's had way better runs than the one he did today, he just doesn't remember them. I shouldn't know that, but I do, because anytime someone at school talked about Landon, my ears would perk up.

The curse of an ex-girlfriend is having radar like that. I've spent an excruciating year keeping tabs on him.

"So where's this girlfriend you mentioned?" his mom asks. "I'm looking forward to meeting her."

I purse my eyes shut, willing this conversation to drop. But I am a teeny bit intrigued about what he may have told her about me.

"She's around here somewhere. You'll really like her," Landon says. "I think she's just putting her horse away. We could walk to the stables. It's a little cooler in the shade."

"That sounds good. I've gotta head out soon, anyway. I'm touring a winery with the girls this afternoon."

Thank God for wineries. If I can just stay hidden, then crisis averted. I can't believe I didn't think about his mom by now, but this could've happened before. On the phone. I'm lucky he's way more into texting and that the reception in the cabins is so spotty.

I slink along the concession stand as they turn back the way I just came.

"I know Mackenzie wants to meet you," Landon says.

His mom stops abruptly, narrowing her eyes as she looks at her son. My heart skips a beat. *Oh, no . . .*

"Mackenzie? But isn't that the same—"

"Hi!" I practically shout, leaping away from the shadows around the stand.

I have no idea what else I can possibly say, but as I step closer to them, I'm confident it has to be *something.* "It's so nice to, uh . . ." *Meet you?* I can't say that. If she remembers my name, then she knows I've met her before. "Uh, so nice to know that you, uh, made it!"

Ugh.

When I basically leap into her arms, she halfheartedly hugs me back. My cheeks burn, but I'm not sure what else to do. "I just heard you say that you've gotta take off, but please let me and Landon walk you to your car," I say, gesturing toward the parking lot, my hands flying all over the place.

Chill. Don't blow it.

His mom glances between us, but when I step toward where I hope to find her car—quickly—she and Landon start to follow, so I keep going. My heart hammers harder in my chest. I can only act like an idiot for so long before Landon's going to wonder what is wrong with me.

"Landon!" a voice calls out. I whirl around, and the relief is strong and swift. It's Bailey, rushing toward us. "I'm so sorry," she says, her eyes wide, "but I *really* need your help with something. Do you have a minute?"

He hesitates. I know he doesn't want to bail on her so soon after their reunion, so I jump in. "Oh, that's totally fine. I can walk your mom out," I say.

When she hesitates, I take it a step further, grabbing her hand and putting it on my elbow, like this is 1852 and she needs a formal escort.

"We *really, really* need your help," Bailey adds.

There's a heartbeat of silence and I hold my breath, feeling totally awkward with his mom holding on to my arm.

"Go ahead, dear," she says, pulling away from me. "We'll catch up some other time."

Thank God. I try not to let my shoulders sag in relief.

"Um, okay. Sorry we didn't get to hang out," he says, hugging his mom.

"It's fine, Landon. Last year you were pretty busy too. I really just came to see your events."

"Okay then!" I burst out, before Landon can respond to her *last year* remark. I pray that somehow he dismisses the comment. "Shall we?"

Bailey grabs Landon by the hand and drags him away, and as he leaves earshot, I find myself breathing again. His mom follows me across the big open driveway, toward a field that has been set up as a parking lot for the out-of-towners.

"Mackenzie," his mother says, as we step into the sparse grass.

"Yes?" I say, leading the way toward her red SUV.

"Why does Landon think I've never met you?" she asks, just as we arrive at her car.

Dang it. "Um, we have? I guess I forgot," I say, giving her my most bashful look. "I mean, it's completely my fault. He thought we'd met before, but I told him we hadn't. I have a really bad memory."

She narrows her eyes and my blood pressure rises a few notches. "And yet you remembered this was my car," she says, jutting her thumb at her SUV.

Oh, crap.

"Um, well . . ." My voice trails off and I look around the lot, as if someone will be holding up a sign with whatever dialog I'm supposed to say next. I can't let his *mom* ruin this summer. Two weeks of this, and it's about to go down the tubes. I haven't nearly *begun* to figure out what I want to do next. I only know the idea of Landon figuring things out, then leaving me in the dust a second time, sends a painful hollowness swooping through my chest.

"See, Landon and I did date last summer," I say. "As you know," I add. I want to cringe, but I can't. I just nod, like what I'm saying makes so much sense, and then I wait for the words to form. "And even though we like each other very much, we had a hard time maintaining our relationship once we got back to school. I'm trying to . . ." To what? "Um, get into the Ivy League. Which I did. I got accepted to Harvard," I say.

Lies. Such lies. I don't even know if it's going to cement into something, but for some absurd reason I've decided she'll be more likely to believe me if I'm going to Harvard. *Stupid, stupid, stupid.* "And it was really hard for me to study for the SATs and everything and maintain our relationship, and Landon has so much going on too. He was working on his WSU applications and his rodeos. So we broke up."

"Uh-huh . . . ," she says. Because I still haven't explained why Landon thinks I've never met his mom before, I'm just babbling like an idiot, waiting for it all to clarify in my head.

"And then when we got back to this ranch, see . . ." I chew on my lip. "We decided to enjoy the summer together. Like last year. So we wiped the slate clean." I mimic an eraser on a chalkboard, except it's way too theatrical, my arm waving around in a giant circular motion that would knock her out if she leaned in the slightest bit.

I can't tell if she's buying what I'm selling, so I surge ahead. "We're pretending this summer is our first summer together, so that we don't bring any . . ." I pause. "Any, uh, baggage to the relationship."

And then I nod at least a half dozen times, like some sort of yes man, and hope it makes more sense to her than it does to me.

She eyeballs me, playing with her keys, and I think I've ruined it all. "That's . . . romantic," she says.

"You think?" I ask, the surprise evident in my tone. Bailey is right. I'm not a good schemer.

"Of course," she says slowly. "Forgiveness is a beautiful thing."

I nod again. "Exactly. So if you could just . . . go along with this, and not question Landon, that would be such a big help to us. We really just want to enjoy this last summer before college. I mean, since I'm going to Harvard," I say, trying to keep a straight face, "we'll probably have to break up again, so that *each of us* can focus on our studies. I wouldn't want to distract him from his future, and it'll be long distance. . . ."

She's nodding like everything I've said makes perfect sense, and I know it has more to do with me promising her that he's going to focus on school than anything else. And just like that, I realize I have my golden ticket.

"Thank you so much. This summer really means so much to us. A bit of fun before we really hunker down and get to work this fall."

And then his mom hugs me, and I hug her back, the relief so strong I almost collapse in her arms.

"Okay then, dear, you just treat him right," she says. "You've got a good head on your shoulders."

And then I smile at her and say, "He will get everything he deserves."

I just wish I knew what that was anymore.

CHAPTER TWENTY-ONE

The evening of the rodeo, I'm lying on the couch, my legs curled over the back of it and my head draped down toward the floor, watching Bailey slide shimmery blue eye shadow over her lids. Upside down, the blue seems bright, but I know she's only half done. There will be blending and smudging and smokiness, until it's artfully perfect, the kind of makeup shown on pull-out magazine ads for Covergirl or MAC cosmetics.

We've both just showered off the grime of a long day's work, and after the two minutes it took me to get ready, sliding on some comfortable jean shorts and a tank top, then putting my hair up in a high, messy bun, I'm stuck waiting for Bailey. Watching her routine upside down makes it no less boring, but there's no way she'll rush it. I could announce that an asteroid is going to hit the ranch in four minutes, and she'd still use the next three and a half to finish her eye shadow.

"At the rate you're going, we'll miss the fireworks," I say, staring up at the swirling blades of the ceiling fan. I'm not sure why we bothered turning it on. It's just circulating hot air.

"Will not," she says.

"They start in twenty minutes," I say.

"I only need two," she says, indignant.

"Right."

She snaps her compact shut, but I know not to get excited, because she just digs around and finds another one. "You can't rush perfection," she says, predictably.

"Yeah, but can you rush mediocre? You're not going to see this guy again in a week, so does it matter if your eye shadow only blends *two* colors?"

"It's red, white, and blue, not white and blue." She makes a weird face in the mirror, her eyes half-closed so she can get a closer look at the eye shadow. "By the way, I pulled out all of the stops today, and Adam barely reacted."

"Do I want to know what 'all the stops' entails?" I ask, tapping my feet on the wall.

"Oh, you know. Brushing against him as I reached for a pen. Leaning forward a little to show off my boobs. Giggling and smiling a lot."

I laugh. "What happened to brilliance?"

"Tried that too. It's hard to have a brilliant conversation with yourself. He was giving me *nothing* to work with."

"Maybe you've simply found the one guy in the entire world not interested in you."

"Not possible," she says, dragging a mascara wand through her lashes. "I even tried the old standby: jealousy."

"What do you mean?"

"Well, you saw my date for tonight, right?"

I nod. Bailey and I ran into him in the driveway at the end of the day.

"He came by the booth earlier, and Adam was there. So I introduced him. And then I gave him a little kiss."

"You did not," I say.

"I did. Classic move, except Adam didn't react to seeing me with Todd. It was really weird." She grins. "Anyway, how did your buckle prank go?"

I frown. "It totally backfired."

"How?"

"Turns out the buckle isn't really a lucky charm. It was his dad's."

"Ouch," she says.

"Yeah, I felt like such a jerk."

"Well, the point of all this was to hit him where it hurts. So you did that even more than you realized. That's not so bad, is it?"

"I don't know, I never wanted to hurt him *that* badly. You should have seen him. He was totally coming undone."

She freezes, a mascara wand halfway to her face, and then stands upright again, turning to face me. I spin around and drop my feet to the floor, pausing as the blood rushes back into my brain.

"What?"

"You changed your mind, didn't you?"

"What? No."

"So you're not seriously thinking about your fake little relationship becoming a real one again."

"Of course not," I lie. "I wouldn't be that stupid."

She stares at me for a few more heartbeats, and I pray she can't see through me.

"Good. Because that would be a huge mistake."

"I know." God, did I know.

I'm saved from any further discussion by a knock at the door. Standing, I smooth back any remaining flyaways from my ponytail, then cross the room and pull the door open.

"Hey," Landon says, grinning at me. He's changed too. Now he looks more like the boy I watch at school every day, wearing a worn, comfortable hunter-green T-shirt with jeans that fit him more loosely and a big silver watch I haven't seen in weeks. He leans against the doorjamb, glancing in at Bailey and then back at me.

"You can come in," Bailey says from somewhere behind me. "Unless Mack prefers to let in as many flies as possible."

"Oh. Um, right." I move aside so Landon can step into our little cabin. His scent comes with him—fresh and clean, like soap and shaving cream, although I'm not sure if he actually shaves. I want to lean into him, let it all envelop me, and then ask him.

"I talked Vic, the mechanic guy, into loaning me a golf cart," he says, grinning and jingling a single key on a big red ring. "He just fixed something on it so I convinced him it needed a thorough test."

"Seriously?" Bailey turns away from the mirror. "That rocks."

"Yep. Your carriage awaits."

"Awesome. In that case let's go before he changes his mind." She drops the makeup case onto the little table with a clatter, plunks down on the sofa, and pulls her electric-blue heels on. Even I have to admit, she looks pretty hot, in a black leather skirt and flowing blue top. She's smart enough to know the miniskirt shows off plenty of skin without a plunging neckline. Girl knows how to work it. Maybe I'll try out her style sometime. For a day. "We just need to swing by cabin twenty-four for my date."

"Isn't that—" Landon starts.

"A guest cabin," she says, waving her hand like it is no big deal. Dating guests isn't something addressed in the rule book, but we all know it is kinda frowned on. If Mr. Ramsey knew how much the guests *liked* Bailey's flirtations, he'd probably pay her better. She probably turned a menial week on a ranch into a fun, flirty little fling. "Yeah. Top of the hill. Let's go."

Landon looks like he's going to say something but I nudge his arm and give him a don't-ask expression, and he just shrugs and turns around, leading the way out into the night.

It's not dark yet, but the moon is rising above the rolling hills, and the air doesn't hold quite the oppressive heat it did just an hour ago, although the cement walkway still radiates the warmth of the day. The air feels perfect against my bare legs and shoulders, and with my hair up like it is, the gentle breeze on the back of my neck is blissful.

We follow him to the cart, and I climb on next to him, the plastic cool against my legs, while Bailey jumps on a seat facing backward. "I swear, Landon, if you make me tumble to the dirt, you're dead."

"I know, I know. We can't have you looking like less than a princess for your date with Richie Rich."

"How did you—" she starts.

"He's a freaking guest, Bailey," I interrupt. "He's obviously rich. The pony on his polo shirt was like six inches tall, and you know what they say: the bigger the emblem, the more expensive the shirt."

"That can't be a thing."

"I'm pretty sure it is," I say. "I read it on Wikipedia."

"Huh. Well, he probably *is* pretty rich. I heard his parents invented Toaster Strudels," Bailey says.

"Wait, that's from a movie!" I say, nearly bouncing out of my seat. "I'm so proud of you."

"Don't get all excited," Bailey says. "It's from *Mean Girls*."

"Hey, that counts as a horror movie as far as I'm concerned," Landon says.

Bailey rolls her eyes as Landon pulls out, driving next to the walkway, in the sparse grass around the workers' cabins, following it until it turns to thick, vivid green as we drive up the hill toward cabin 24.

It's way bigger than the humble home for Bailey and me. It has six-foot-wide windows on either side of the big wooden-and-glass front door, and a large porch houses a swing and a small bistro set for breakfast dining.

"I'll be right back," Bailey says, bounding off the cart and toward the cabin as soon as we pull to a stop. We watch in silence as she knocks on the door. When it opens, it isn't quite light enough to see who answers, and she slips inside and the door clicks shut.

"So, should we just wait while they hook up, or—"

"Hey," I say, smacking his chest. "They're not hooking up in there. He's probably not ready to go yet."

"Mm-hmm . . . ," he says, his lips curling into an irresistible smile. He taps his fingers on the steering wheel, and I'm not quite sure what to say next.

"I know she's a little boy crazy, but she has her reasons."

"And those reasons would be?"

"I'm not telling *you* that," I say.

"Why not? I thought girls told their boyfriends everything."

"Not *everything*. I'm sure you have your secrets."

His finger drumming falters before picking up right where it left off. "Nope. No secrets here. Pretty much a what-you-see-is-what-you-get kinda guy."

I twist around and stare at him. "Everyone has secrets."

"Oh yeah? What's yours then, Nancy Drew?"

My mouth goes dry. I only have one, and if he figures it out, I'll lose him before I even figure out what I actually *want* from him.

The door flies open and Bailey bounds out, her latest boy toy in tow. He grins and waves at us as they approach.

"Okay, Todd, this is my friend Mack and her boyfriend, Landon."

"Nice to meet you," I say, giving him a little wave.

"Same here," Todd says. "And, uh, I brought refreshments." He holds up the small cooler in his hand, shaking it around and rattling the ice.

Landon reaches out and the two fist bump. "Awesome. Hop on, and we'll head over the hill."

Bailey and Todd climb onto the backseat, and Todd puts the cooler between his feet, sliding over and throwing his arm loosely around Bailey's shoulders. She leans in and whispers something, and I can tell even from behind he's grinning.

God, I want to be more like her and less like the sniveling girl who is actually considering getting back with the guy who dumped her.

Landon drives up the grassy knoll, and at the crest, he lets off the gas, just as the rolling green hills unfold before us. The view of the golf course never gets old. The sprinklers are on, *skit-skit-skit*ting across the emerald-green lawns.

"You guys don't mind getting a teeny bit wet, do you?" Landon asks, but he doesn't wait for an answer before hitting the gas again. We bound down the hill, the little golf cart motor making a low humming noise as we pick up speed. He's battling a grin and losing.

I turn just in time to get blasted by a sprinkler—straight to the face.

He bursts out laughing and the cart speeds past, my shirt now dripping wet.

"Landon!" I say, wiping the water from my nose and cheeks, then wringing out my shirt.

"What? I warned—"

Bailey shrieks as another sprinkler whips around and hits her side and legs. I whirl around and look at the sprinkler, real-izing it was barely hitting the path at all.

"You're doing this on purpose!" I say, poking his arm.

His lips tremble with a smile. " 'You're doomed! You're all doomed!' "

"Friday the 13th," I say, recognizing not just the words but the weird way he's saying them. But before I can say anything else, another blast of cool water hits my bare legs. I reach over and grab the steering wheel, veering it to the left so that a

sprinkler on the other side of the path just skims across his ankles.

"I'm driving! You totally can't do that!" His laughter, low and deep, says otherwise. I push harder on the steering wheel and even though I know he's much stronger than me, he must be playing fair because the cart dodges to the left again. A sprinkler hits the entire side of the cart, so that both Todd and Landon are blasted across their arms and shoulders.

Landon grins at me, a smile of pure, unadulterated glee. The kind I would trust if I didn't know better. He turns us back onto the path, and I glance around, looking for the next sprinkler. But just as I see it, Landon hits the brakes, and the cart skids to a stop.

I realize a heartbeat too late what he's up to.

"Ahhhh!" Bailey and I shriek and leap from the cart because he's stopped at the perfect spot so that we're being drenched in a torrential blast of water.

I dash around the cart and hide on the other side, shoving Landon with all my might into the passenger seat, but he doesn't move.

Instead, he stands and, before I can turn and run, he picks me up and throws me over his shoulder. I have no time to react, struggle, grab the cart—anything, really—before he's jogging across the lawn and sprinklers are hitting me on all sides.

"Okay, okay, okay! Put me down!" I'm breathless with laughter, soaked to the bone, and . . .

Loving every minute.

He gently sets me back on my feet. I kick off my flip-flops and enjoy the cool, moist grass against my skin. "I bet I can beat you to the sand trap," I say, pointing to the peanut-shaped white sand just down the hill. The entire hillside is lined with sprinklers, and we'll be soaked all over again before we reach the trap.

"You're on," he says, kicking off one flip-flop.

Before the second one is off his foot, I sprint away, half-heartedly dodging the sprinklers as I go, squealing when one spins around and blasts the backs of my legs.

The grass is slick and I slow as I descend toward the sand trap, but then there's Landon, running by.

No, not running past me. He grabs my hand and we're running down the slope together, the night air cool against my wet skin and clothes. Behind us, Todd and Bailey are laughing, jumping through the sprinklers as if this was the plan all along.

We reach the sand and half slide to a stop. I'm breathing hard and so is Landon—his T-shirt, now drenched, clings to every muscle and curve of his shoulders. My own T-shirt is practically see-through, to the point that Landon must be able to see the dark outline of my black bra, but I can't bring myself to be embarrassed.

We face each other, and the smile slips from my face as I see the intensity of his look. He steps toward me, cupping his hands around the back of my neck, and pulls me to him.

I'm breathless as our lips touch for the first time in nearly a year. His are soft, warm, so perfect, that I find myself leaning into it, the world around us disappearing. It's him and me and the night and nothing more.

And then the fireworks explode above us.

We pull apart, just enough so that he can wrap his arm

around me, and we look up at the now-dark night sky as red and white explode into a star-shaped formation.

"Let's find a patch of dry grass," he says, his breath hot as he talks, so close to my skin. I nod.

He leads me away from the sand trap until we're on the other side, where the sprinklers aren't currently running. They'll probably turn on next, but I can't bring myself to care.

We find a soft flat spot and stretch out side by side. He puts his arm under my head, and I cradle into him, staring up at the sky as a flash of green spirals across the night. I want the moment to last forever. I want to fall asleep out here, in his arms, staring at the night sky.

In this instant, everything clarifies.

I want desperately for him to fall in love with me, for this relationship to last beyond the fall, beyond the few short weeks it did last year.

I want forever.

"It's beautiful," I say after a few heartbeats of silence.

"Yeah. It's better than I imagined," he says.

And as purple explodes above him, I wonder if he means the fireworks or being with me.

CHAPTER TWENTY-TWO

I'm in Landon's cabin, waiting as he showers, because he invited me over to watch a horror movie. Together. Alone. Like we did last year. Except last year it was always some generic blockbuster we borrowed from Bailey's collection, and we always ended up making out.

It feels weird, being in here waiting for him. Like it's too intimate, listening to the water run and imagining . . .

No, not imagining. I shake my head. I refuse to imagine. *"Danger, Will Robinson,"* I think, *imagining Landon naked will only . . .*

Dang it, I'm thinking about it again.

I sit up straighter and cross my legs at the ankle, as if proper posture will clean out my thoughts too. I glance around the room, taking in the standard-issue couch, small fridge, and cupboards. The only personal effects are the Seahawks throw blanket tossed over the couch, a magazine about classic cars and trucks on the coffee table, and a small stack of DVDs on top of the TV.

His phone chirps, and I lean over to where it sits on the side table. It's a text from his sister, something about a soccer game.

But seeing it gives me an idea. My feelings for Landon might have shifted, but this little prank war of ours—except for the disastrous buckle incident—is too fun to give up. I pick up the phone as I realize he hasn't locked the screen. I tap on the Facebook icon and the empty white box pops up, the cursor blinking at me. Then I close the app and grab an image off of Google, swapping out his main header image for one of six kittens in a little basket with flowers. Then I find every Justin Bieber–centric fan page possible in under thirty seconds, liking all of them, and changing his religion from blank to "Belieber."

I pause, listening to the running water. May as well keep rolling. I open his contacts list and start editing. Mom becomes Effie Trinket; Mike, his buddy from auto shop, is turned into Peeta Mellark; his sisters become Katniss and Primrose; some random girl named Trina becomes Tribute From District 7. By the time I'm done, every number on the list has become a character from *The Hunger Games*.

But when I scroll further and see Natalie, my heart skips a beat.

Natalie. She's still in his contact list.

I'm positive they're not together anymore—I heard she was dating this guy named Barrett, from White River High School, but I don't think it matters. I know how he worked last time. He enjoyed our fun little summer fling. I fell hard, and he moved on.

Somehow it has to be different this time.

So I change her contact name to Seneca Crane, then put the

phone back to sleep and set it on the little table. Landon steps out of the bathroom a moment later.

"Sorry that took so long," he says.

"Not a problem," I say. "I didn't even notice."

"Great. I have an idea," he says, rubbing the towel over his hair before tossing it onto a nearby chair. He's now wearing shorts and no shirt and I force myself to look at his face and nowhere else.

"Oh?"

"Yeah. What do you say we ditch the movie idea and just sneak into the spa?"

"Why would we do that?"

"Hot tub. Duh."

Hot tub. Hot. Oy, I should not be nodding my head. "Yeah, that sounds . . . kinda amazing. I'm totally sore from riding."

"Awesome." He picks up the remote and clicks the TV off.

"Let me grab us some towels and put on my swim trunks. I'll meet you over at your cabin in a few minutes," he says.

"Sounds good," I say, heading out the door. Once out of sight of his windows, I grin. I have another idea. I hustle down the path, winding around to my cabin. I stop at the door and tap twice, just in case Bailey's inside doing her own little dirty deeds, but she hollers, "Come in."

She's sitting cross-legged on the couch, her iPad in her lap. "Hey," she says without looking up. I can tell even from the side, however, that she's wearing some kind of goopy purple mask.

"What is that crap?" I ask, walking over to the kitchen and grabbing a glass of water.

"Something my mom sent in a care package. A deep mois-turizing, clarifying mask or something."

"Ahh." I stare a moment longer.

"Why are you back so early?" She taps away at the screen, and something explodes in a dazzling show of lights. She whispers *yesss* under her breath. She must be winning.

"I'm not back yet. Landon wants to sneak into the spa and use the hot tub."

Her eyes finally snap up to meet mine. "Sexy."

"Yeah. Huh. I guess," I say, acting as if every thought I've had of him in the last sixty seconds can't be summed up with that one word. *Sexy.* Yes.

She's back to tapping at the screen. "Have you pranked him lately?"

"I used his phone while he was in the shower and changed all his contacts to the cast of *The Hunger Games*, so yeah."

"Brilliant. But kind of . . . benign?"

"What makes you think I'm done yet?"

She quirks a brow, then slides the iPad off her lap and stands. "I've just decided that you are definitely wearing that new white bikini I bought in town."

I picture the tiny little thing she picked out in the boutique we visited a few days ago. "By white bikini, you mean mass of tangled strings, right?"

"Something like that." She disappears into her room.

And even though I know I should object, I follow.

A few minutes later, Landon and I are walking the path to the spa, hand in hand.

"So, zombies," I say.

"Zombies?"

"Yeah. If they ever become a real thing, what do you think is the most likely cause? Virus or genetic mutation?"

"Easy. Virus."

Dang. I was hoping he'd go with genetic mutation, because I actually agree that a virus makes more sense.

"No way," I say. "With all the genetically engineered crap these days, mutation is way more likely."

"With all the genetically engineered crap? What about viruses? Every time we turn around there's another bird flu or swine flu and another rushed vaccine to battle it."

"Yeah, but you're talking about changing the very essence of humanity, not giving them the flu. I mean, rotting flesh, scrambled brains? That's got to be genetic."

"Yeah? And how exactly do you think we spontaneously mutate?"

I shrug. "People are already trying to clone themselves or create designer babies. It's only a matter of time before one goes wrong, but since it's a *baby,* they won't kill it off."

"So you think a single baby is going to start the zombie apocalypse."

"I didn't say anything about the apocalypse. Just the existence of a zombie," I say as we approach the back side of the spa. "Huh. I forgot about those prongy things," I say, pointing to the teeth at the top of the swooping iron fence.

"There aren't any at the top of the gates," he says, leading me down the fence line to a pair of gates with pretty iron ivy twirling around the slats. The decor belongs at a winery, but whatever. "And we're tabling this zombie convo, but I'm not letting you off the hook. Your argument is weak."

"Oh, whatever! You just can't admit you're wrong."

He shakes his head. "Not true. And anyway, let me boost you over."

"Um, okay." I eyeball the gate. "But are you sending me first because it's really a ploy to be sure that if there is a laser-guided security system, I'm the one who trips it?"

He snorts. "This isn't a casino or a bank vault or something."

"But they could still have security in place, right?" God I am being such a chicken right now.

"Didn't you ask Bailey this? Or get her key?"

"It didn't occur to me until now. But I've opened the spa with her before and we never turned off any kind of alarm, so . . ."

"Okay then. Here." He squats. "Step on my leg and then into my hands, and I'll push you over. Then you can unlatch the gate."

"Right." I take a deep breath and then grab hold of the iron slats, stepping up onto his knee with my right foot, then into his interlaced hands with my left foot, and then he pushes me up over the gate.

And then I'm dropping onto my feet inside the spa. I pause and survey my surroundings, making sure there isn't a camera I'd never noticed or the blare of a horn. But nothing.

I turn around and hit the latch on the gate.

"See? Easy." He walks in, and I forget to step back to give him space, and then we're inches apart. He leans down and kisses me. I close my eyes until I hear the clang of the gate behind him. He'd reached back and shut it while I was distracted.

"Right, then. Let's go." I lead him around the curving paths. There are a series of irregularly shaped pools, some of them salt water and others regular old chlorinated water.

I lead him to an oval hot tub at the far end, surrounded by bushes on three sides and hidden from just about everything. I always liked this one the best.

Landon yanks off his T-shirt, and I fight the urge to spin around as if it's not appropriate for him to be undressed. This is totally normal. Not at all . . .

I take a deep breath and then pull my shirt over my head, revealing my borrowed itty-bitty string bikini. It's stark white in the darkness, complementing my tanned skin. Without giving myself the time to chicken out, I slide my shorts down and let them drop to the cement pathway.

Landon lets out a low whistle under his breath, and I turn to meet his eyes, taking in his predatory yet appreciative gaze. "You've been holding out on me all summer," he says.

And suddenly I'm *very* glad Bailey talked me into wearing this, because there is no way he's thinking about anything but me. "Good things come to those who wait," I say, and then step to the edge of the hot tub, dipping my toe into the water.

"And to those who think they've waited long enough?"

"I guess we'll find out," I say, smiling coyly at him as I splash the water in his direction with my toe. I'm not sure where this flirty girl came from, but I think I like her.

I lower myself down to the first step at the edge of the spa, then step down again until the water rises up my thighs, then touches my hips. Landon doesn't move to follow me, just watches, his face almost impassive. And then when the water tops my belly button, he finally moves, coming around to the steps where I entered and following me, until we're standing in the middle of the tub. The water hits the bottom of my rib cage, but on Landon it's barely over the spot where his muscles indent around his hips.

I feel warm under the intensity of his gaze, and I let myself touch his arm. He smiles, the barest lifting of his lips revealing those stark white teeth. "You look . . ." I don't fill in the blanks as I want to know what he's about to say. "Delicious."

And then despite the heat of the water, I shiver.

He traces a finger up my arm, drawing little circles on my shoulder before dancing down my collarbone, walking his fingers across my skin and leaving a trail of goose bumps in his wake. He stops at the base of my throat, his fingers whisper-soft. I lick my lips involuntarily, and his gaze darts to my mouth.

"You should really not do that again," he says, his voice low and sultry, and I think I just melted into the hot tub.

Before I even register what I'm doing, I lick my lips again, and in an instant he's crushing me up against him, his hands cupping my jawline on either side as he pulls my face up to meet his.

And then we're kissing and it's a good thing he's holding me like this, because I am certain my legs don't actually exist anymore, that they've left my body to stand on its own.

He moves one hand back and tangles it into my hair, his other arm sliding around behind me, pressing me against him, and I finally wake up enough to move, letting my hands skim up across his abs before resting against his heart.

I'm not sure how long we stand like that, kissing. When we finally pull apart I'm breathless, my head spinning. I thunk down on the hard stone bench that curves around the outer edges of the tub.

Landon sits down a few feet away, and when I meet his eyes I realize he's grinning, ear to ear, a strangely intoxicating mixture of pleasure and arrogance, as if he's simultaneously saying he enjoyed it and that he *knew* I'd enjoyed it as much as he had.

"You are trouble," I say, splashing water toward him.

"Yeah, it's too bad you like me so much," he says.

"Yeah. It's too bad." I nod. "I vote we skinny-dip in that salt-water pool," I say, pointing to the pool that is most concealed by bushes.

"I'm game," he says.

"Okay then," I say, standing. "You go get in first. Then close your eyes and I'll join you."

"No way, you first."

"Uh-uh. No deal. You have to be in the pool so I know you can't see me."

"I never knew you were so modest," he says, but he's getting out of the hot tub, heading toward the saltwater pool. I follow him halfway, then pause next to the bushes.

"I swear I won't peek," I call out, turning around and staring at the backside of the spa building, listening to the sounds of Landon undressing.

"What if I want you to?" There's a playfulness to his tone, and I fight the blush burning in my cheeks, refusing to turn and see him.

When the water splashes and my heartbeat is thundering louder than a summer storm, I call out, "Is it safe to turn around?"

"Uh-huh," he says. When I look back at him, he's in the middle of the pool, the water lapping around his bare shoulders.

I'm glad the night is so dark, because I'm so hardcore blushing right now.

"Okay. Turn around," I say. "So I can ditch my clothes."

He sighs and does as I ask. I wait a heartbeat, staring at the muscles on his back. Then I dash over to the bush, where he's tossed his clothing. "No peeking," I repeat, grabbing his shorts and T-shirt off the shrub, then picking up our towels off the ground.

Part of me doesn't want to go through with this little prank, but I can't possibly get into the pool naked with him. I just can't give him any more power until I know his feelings for me are real.

His back is still to me, so I creep farther away, until I'm standing near the fence line, clutching all of his clothing.

"Have a good night!" I call out, the laughter evident in my voice as I shove my way through the gate.

Water splashes, followed by muttered curse words, but I can't make out his response as I run, barefoot, away from the spa.

CHAPTER TWENTY-THREE

"Are you sure I don't look stupid?" I say, staring into the mirror. I'm wearing Bailey's clothes from head to toe. We don't have the same shoe size, though, so I don't want to know how she found tasseled shoes in my size. "I wanted to make him think I've golfed before, but I seriously look like I'm playing dress up."

"It's classic. Sophisticated."

"It just makes my hair seem even weirder," I say, frowning and tipping my head to the side as I study the extreme contrast of tricolored hair paired with preppy clothes.

Bailey walks past me and grabs a Diet Coke from our fridge. She pops the top and slams the fridge shut with her hip before looking at me again. "The golf course has a dress code, so everyone is going to look like this. Lucky for you, they don't have a hair code. Clearly no one on this entire ranch saw you coming."

"Do you think golf is one of those fake-it-till-you-make-it sports?"

She takes a sip of her soda and stares me down, as if I'm supposed to have some dawning realization or something. Then she says, "No. There's no chance he's going to buy that you've been golfing your whole life. Just act like you've always loved watching it. Be a fan of the sport, since he's into it. Anything more and he's going to see through it."

"Yeah, you're probably right." I stop fiddling with the hem of the short khaki skirt and raise a brow at her. "You know, I kinda look like you."

"Exactly, which is how I know you look so awesome."

I grab the soda from her hands, then down the rest of it before tossing the can into the garbage. "I'm just glad we can use the course for free on our days off. The normal fees are ridiculous."

"I know. Now let's go," she says. "My date is meeting us there and we're already late and it's, like, a million degrees outside, and it's only going to get worse."

I give up protesting, because when she sets her mind to something, there's no contradicting her. Instead, I simply follow her, feeling the tiniest bit like a Bailey clone as we step out into the sunlight. My hair is in two little French braids, and the red and blue aren't quite as overwhelming this way.

Just as I step off the porch, Landon walks up. "You guys are dressed like bona fide yuppies," he says, grinning widely.

I take in his polo shirt, khaki pants, brown leather shoes. "Uh, I'm sorry, I thought my boyfriend was meeting us here. Have you seen him? Texas accent, jeans, boots, and a little cowboy swagger?"

He grins. "Only a little swagger? I'm offended. Truly."

"I can tell," I say drily.

"Can you two stop flirting already? We're running late."

Bailey pushes past us, and Landon gives me a what's-her-deal look. I shrug. We follow her up the pathway, and I half laugh as she stumbles on a tiny little rock and barely catches herself.

"Where's the fire?" I call out, but she just flips me off and keeps walking. A few minutes later, we're at the main entry to the golf course, where guests sign up, find caddies, and get refreshments.

There's a guy standing there, and I realize he's Bailey's date when she walks up and throws her arms around him. Another guy I've never met, never heard of, before today. I mean, sure, last year, Bailey had fun playing the field, flirting up a storm. But this year, it's reached a whole new level.

Michael is . . . cute but a little too conservative. His polo is actually buttoned all the way up, and his hair is gelled within an inch of its life. When he smiles, it's perfectly even, showing off flawless straight teeth. "Hey," he says to us with a wave.

"Hey. You must be Michael," I say, sticking out my hand. "Bailey told me all about you."

It's a lie, but oh well. He shakes my hand. "Nice to meet you."

Landon introduces himself and shakes Michael's hand.

"So, I already signed us in. There's a group on the first hole, and then we're up next."

"Awesome. Did you want to practice your shot first?" Landon asks, turning to me. "We can use the driving range."

Right. Like it'll just take a couple of practice swings for me to be ready for the full course. If we'd shared a PE class last year, he'd know better.

"Nah, I'm more of a dive into the deep end kind of girl," I say. "I mean, I'm pretty terrible, but I *love* golf, don't you?"

He beams. "Yeah, definitely."

I knew that. How did people ever scheme before social networking and high school yearbooks?

"Yep, dive into the deep end, that's me too," Bailey says. "Every time I golf, I like to just jump right into the first hole."

We share a smile, because I know her golf game is going to be just as hopeless as my own.

"Okay, then. We have two sets of clubs, so if you don't mind sharing, let's get going," Michael says.

"Good with me," I say. We follow the boys past the little registration house, heading down a pretty aggregate sidewalk, one that bends and curves around the landscaping.

"I didn't get a cart because frankly I prefer walking," Landon says.

"Absolutely," I say. "Walking is the only way to really experience the game."

"Great. Then let's go golf."

Three hours later, I'm standing in front of the sink in one of the bathrooms positioned around the sprawling course, using a damp paper towel to wipe the back of my neck.

"I think I'm going to melt," Bailey says, running her wrists under cold water.

"I think I already did," I respond, tossing the napkin into the nearby trash bin. "Remind me why we have to finish the last two holes?"

"Because you're supposed to make Landon think you're loving every minute of this," she says. "And because Michael wants to."

"And since when do you do crap you don't want to do just for a guy? Obviously that's more my style," I say, gesturing to my borrowed clothes.

"That's a good point, but I'm not sure how to get out of it," she says. "Plus, I decided about two hours ago I'm not even into him."

I literally scratch my head. "Then why haven't we bailed yet?"

"Because the one guy I'm actually into, like *really* into, as in I can't stop thinking about him, isn't interested."

My mouth drops open. Bailey's spent the last year and a half trying to convince me that guys are interchangeable. "And that guy is . . ."

"Adam," she says miserably. "I've tried every trick in the book, and he acts like I'm not even there!"

"You could consider, you know, just asking him out." I wipe my hands on a paper towel, then toss it into the garbage as we head to the door.

"I don't know how," she says, and it's so hilarious I almost laugh out loud. "*He*'s supposed to ask *me* out, but I've done everything in my power and *nothing*."

"Are you sure you're not into him just because he's resisted your charms? Thrill of the chase or whatever?"

"It's not that. I mean, okay, maybe it was at first."

I wait.

"But while trying to scheme and flirt my way into a date, I started to notice all these things about him. He's . . . smart and funny but super sweet too. After we shut down the ticket booth at the rodeo we were walking back toward the cabins and he overheard this girl say she really wanted cotton candy. She was a dollar short and he dug out a five and handed it to her without a word. You should have seen her expression! He was her hero."

"So you're telling me your love can be bought for five dollars," I joke.

Bailey smacks my arm. "No, I can be impressed by adorable, selfless gestures. You know he's basically terrified of horses? But he heard them say they needed help and that's how he got stuck leading them in. And he's the first generation in his family to go to college. And did you notice that the shower in our cabin is draining way better? I mentioned it and *bam,* he was there to fix it, just because I said it bugged me."

"Okay, okay, he's your dream man. I'm convinced."

"You're so annoying," she says. "Don't you get how sometimes you just *know* a guy is amazing? That's him."

As we step back into the hot glare of the noon sun, the laughter dies in my throat. Landon and Michael are standing in the shade of a nearby tree, and Adam's walking toward us, pushing a big cart with shovels and boxes on it. "Incoming," I whisper to Bailey. And then I turn to Adam. "Hey," I say. "Is it hot out here or *what?*"

He takes off his hat and wipes the sweat from his brow. "Yeah. I started at dawn, and with every hour I think I'm dying a little more."

"Will you be done soon?" I ask, glancing at Bailey. "We were thinking of going swimming later. If you don't have, like, princesses to save or whatever."

Bailey blinks, then recovers. "Yeah, you should join us. I'll be your princess and, you never know, I might be in distress and need, like, mushrooms or something."

Oh God, it's all I can do not to slap my hand over her mouth.

"Uh, yeah," he says, extra-slow, like he's not sure what to make of Bailey's statement. "Swimming sounds great. I've got two more sprinklers to replace. Can we go in a couple of hours?"

"Sure," Bailey says.

Adam grabs the handles to his cart. "Okay, then. Meet you guys around four?"

"Yeah. See you then," I say, leading Bailey away.

She catches up to me and says, "God, it's like I can't turn off my flirty ditz mode! *Mushrooms?* It was all silly and playful when you did it, and I sound like an idiot! What is wrong with me?"

"I don't know, but he's not into it."

"Thanks, I noticed," she says drily.

"You have another chance later," I say, walking toward Landon and Michael. I lower my voice. "We just have to get rid of Michael first."

"So, we were thinking," Landon says, "that we should ditch the last two holes and go swimming. You guys in?"

I dart a look at Bailey. "Uh, no," I say, scrambling for a way to keep Michael from going swimming later. "I'm super determined to make it through the whole course, and plus the river is really gross right now. Uh, storm water runoff. From, like, Idaho. It's all over the news."

Landon furrows his brow, staring between me and Bailey.

I elbow her.

"Uh, yeah," she says. "And I really want to finish this course. I feel like I'm starting to catch on."

"Okaaaay then," Michael says slowly. "Let's get these last two holes done."

He walks away, and I lean into Bailey as we follow. "You so owe me big-time. I think I've lost ten pounds from sweating, and I just volunteered for more of this crap."

She smiles. "Thank you."

Two hours later, our discarded clothes are piled high on the rock near the edge of the water. I'm wearing Bailey's string bikini again, with a pair of pink shorts, and Bailey's wearing her more modest one-piece, except it has a big diamond-shaped cutout over her belly button. I convinced her less was more when it came to Adam, and I'm pretty sure I'm right. I've caught him checking her out twice now. Her hair's in a messy ponytail, and since she couldn't find her waterproof mascara, she washed it off and looks a little more au naturel than usual. He seems more into her.

She's standing hip-deep in the water, and Adam's teaching her how to skip rocks. She sucks at it, but she can't stop trying. Every time she screws up, he laughs, but she's not embarrassed. Instead, she's got this glow I don't usually see, because she's enjoying herself instead of playing coy or sexy or whatever.

Landon and I stand hip-deep in the water, and I let my palm skim the surface. "This feels so freaking good," I say. "I don't know why we didn't do this in the first place."

"Golfing was your idea," he says. "And so was finishing the course."

"Um, yeah, but I didn't realize how hot it would get," I say. "And Bailey finally got Adam to hang out, so we had to finish the course in order to ditch Michael. Besides, you looked like you were enjoying it."

"I like golf. I was on the golf team at school last year, you know."

"Of course I knew that," I say. It's the only reason I'd suggested golf for today.

"Good. I mean, *I* know you're in FBLA, little Miss Future Business Leader of America."

My eyes widen without my meaning them to. He's talking about two years ago, before we'd ever come to this ranch. He'd noticed me at school? "How?"

"You sell raffle tickets at their table. You're kinda hard to miss, with your sexy little miniskirts and orange leggings, yelling about changing the world, signing petitions, donating money. The other girls kinda sit there like bumps on a log, but you, you went after it. I saw you throw a packet at Kenny Miller once, and it hit him in the face, yet you didn't look embarrassed. More . . . smug. And dang if I didn't watch him donate ten bucks."

I laugh. That had actually happened. I'd been getting so annoyed after a long lunch period of being ignored, and his group was standing in a big cluster in front of our table, blocking our signs from view. I'd tried three times to get his attention and he'd ignored me, so I threw a *Save Our Local Rivers* pamphlet right at him, except I accidently nailed him in the face.

"So if you noticed me, why'd you never talk to me at school?"

I want to ask a more pointed question—I want to ask him why he ignored me after last summer, why he had to act like I didn't exist, but I couldn't.

"I would've eventually," he says. "But we never had classes together."

He's wrong, though. We had senior English together, the most miserable hour of my every day. I stared at the back of his head for those sixty minutes, willing him to turn around, willing him to just *explain* how he could drop me and move on so fast.

"Plus I was a little worried for my safety."

I laugh again and splash water at him.

"What? You've got a heck of an arm," he says, splashing water right back. "You could poke my eye out or something."

"It's not too late, I could still poke your eye out," I say, stepping closer. I push hard on his bare chest, but he just grabs my wrists and slips them up over his shoulders, yanking me against him. I let my feet leave the ground, wrapping my legs around him, but I realize too late I've given up control.

He buckles his legs and we go under. I want to let go, push away, swim frantically toward the surface, because I've barely gotten in a lungful of air, but he's still holding me. So I wait, my eyes shut.

And just as my lungs scream for air, he stands again, and my head pops over the surface.

"You're a jerk," I say.

"But an irresistible one, right?"

"Maybe."

"Say yes, or we're going under again," he says, bobbling a little, so the water slides up my stomach again.

"Okay, okay," I mutter.

"Say it," he says, ducking a little.

"You're irresistible."

CHAPTER TWENTY-FOUR

"Are you sure these aren't, like, used?" Bailey whispers. "Because that would be totally gross."

"Yeah, I'm sure," I say, rubbing the sore tip of my finger. "They were in a big box and it was still sealed shut."

"Where the heck did you even find a box of fifty mouse-traps?" Bailey asks, leaning back against the big cedar pillar behind her.

I shake the tingling pain out of my hand. These things are trickier than I thought. I've already snapped my fingers twice, and each time my heart roared to life, worried the noise had carried into Landon's bedroom. He *cannot* wake up.

At least, not yet.

"Costco?" I guess. We're sitting on the front steps of Landon's cabin, in the light of the moon, setting up the traps one by one. We've been here twenty minutes, and with each passing moment,

I feel a little more wound up, like the coils on our silly traps. "I mean, I didn't get them from the store or anything. I talked Adam into opening up one of those maintenance sheds behind the golf shop."

"Oh," she says, yawning. "I'm going to be so tired tomorrow." She sets another trap down on the tray, next to a half dozen others.

"I know, I know. But this is so going to be worth it." I reach into my pocket and slide out my cell phone, blinking against the bright glare of light. "We have six more minutes before the alarm goes off. Forty-two is probably good enough," I say.

"Great because my fingers hurt," she says, setting down the trap in her hand.

I have no idea how I could've gotten all this done without her. "You're kind of the best friend in the entire universe, you know that, right?"

"I know." She grins at me. "And if I ever hatch some insane revenge scheme on an ex-boyfriend, you better be right there with me."

I turn away abruptly when she says "revenge scheme," my cheeks warming. I haven't really told her that I'm not sure I want revenge anymore.

I want Landon instead.

"Uh, Mack, what's with that look?"

"What look?" I ask, not meeting her eyes as I set another trap.

"That weird look you got when I said revenge. This is still about revenge, right?"

I purse my lips.

"Right?"

"Um . . ."

"You *cannot* change the plan, Mack. That will end badly. Very, very badly."

"How can you be so sure, though? He's different now." I stare at the ground, willing her to agree, to validate my feelings.

Our relationship isn't the same this time around. It's just not. And I need her to say so too, so that it's not all in my head.

"That doesn't mean he's in love with you for real. I mean we wanted him to fall, but it's not like we thought he'd become boyfriend material even if he did. He's not that kind of guy."

"I think you're wrong," I say, my throat suddenly feeling raw. "I think he has real feelings. And weirdly, despite all our scheming, I feel like he gets me."

"Yeah? And when you get to WSU, and another girl catches his eye, what then? Do you really want to walk into some building and see him making out with another girl again?"

"It's not the same."

"It is, and you know it." She stares right into my eyes. "Mack, even if he did fall, you'd have to tell him what you've been up to all summer. He's not going to take kindly to you making a fool of him. When he knows what we've done, he'll just bail."

I rake in a jagged breath of air. "I don't know, I need to think about it more. I guess I'm just confused," I say.

"You better get *un*confused before he rips out your heart again."

"I know," I say. "And anyway, I'm still pranking him, aren't I? He's going to hate this."

I hope she doesn't see the fear and the apprehension and a million other emotions probably swirling in my eyes.

"You got it." We stand, each of us picking up one of the lunch trays we jacked from the cafeteria. Only about a dozen traps fit on the surface, so we'll have to make a couple of trips.

I thank the ranch gods who gave Landon this cabin, at the end of the sidewalk, partially hidden by the big weeping willow. If someone had spotted us, I'm not sure how I could explain me and Bailey sitting on his porch setting forty-two mousetraps.

I step carefully over the two trays still sitting on the the front porch, turning back to Bailey to give her the *shhhhh* signal before putting my hand on the doorknob. For one soul-crushing moment I think Landon, for once in his life, actually bothered to lock the door, but then it clicks and we're inside. We slide off our flip-flops near the door, then step noiselessly forward, into his living room. I lead her toward the bedroom, glancing back one more time to be sure she's not about to trip on the rug and ruin our little plans. She's following, her eyes trained on her lunch tray.

We make tiny, silent movements as we approach his bed. He's sprawled out on his stomach, his head turned away from us, the blanket kind of mounded over him, moonlight spilling in through the slats of his blinds.

Perfect.

I pick up a trap around the edges, my hand shaking a little as I lower the mousetrap onto his alarm clock. I don't take another breath until it's resting there and my hand is at my side again. Behind me, Bailey stoops over, setting the traps she brought in down on the ground.

It only takes seconds to slide them off the trays and onto the floor, and I'm straining to discern any difference in his breathing the whole time. It remains deep and even, and he doesn't move an inch.

Bailey and I meet eyes as I place the last trap, and she flashes me a thumbs-up. I nod and follow her back to the door, where we grab the other two trays and return to his room, spreading them out on the floor around the side and foot of his bed. When we're done, I step back and admire our work, my eyes darting to the red digits on Landon's alarm clock.

One minute.

When the clock ticks over and the blare finally comes I almost shriek, even though I'd expected it. Instead I clamp my jaw down and watch as Landon moans, then slowly turns, his blanket twisting around his body.

I hold my breath as he reaches out in the darkness, slamming his fingers down on the trap.

His eyes pop open as he yelps and springs from bed, yanking his hand so hard the trap flies across the room, and I have to duck. It bounces off the wall above my head.

The blankets tangle around his legs and he crashes to the floor, where he sets off a series of traps against his arms, his chest, and his feet. Amidst the *snap-snap-snap-snap,* I burst out laughing, falling over into Bailey as she does the same.

"Argrghghgh," Landon groans as another trap snaps against his arm and then stills. The room falls silent, save the stifled giggles of me and Bailey as I try desperately to get myself back under control. Maybe we should've bailed before he knew it was us, but there was no way I could miss this, and besides, I'm not sure who else would be his prime suspect.

I get my giggles under control just as he speaks.

"Oh man," he says. "I totally underestimated you."

I grin, triumph spinning through my veins. "One, two, I'm

coming for you. Three, four, better lock your door," I say, in a singsong voice. Then I spin on my heel and head for the exit.

"Nightmare on Elm Street," Landon calls after me.

I stop in the doorway, my hand on the knob. "Yep," I say, smiling devilishly.

"Definitely a nightmare," he adds, groaning again as the door slams shut behind me.

CHAPTER TWENTY-FIVE

"How are things going with Adam?" I ask. Bailey and I are sitting cross-legged on the floor of the main dining hall, the one typically used for the guests. The summer is almost over, and we're assembling paper lanterns to be hung at the dance in a couple of days.

She frowns, staring at the directions in her hand as if they're written in Spanish. "He didn't even try to kiss me after our date last night."

I put a glob of glue on a Popsicle stick. There's gotta be a better way to do paper lanterns, like maybe buying them premade, but if Mr. Ramsey wants to pay me and Bailey to sit around constructing these in an air-conditioned building all day, I'm not going to argue.

"A guy can like you and not kiss you, you know. It's called chivalry."

"That's not what that word means," she says. "I'm down with

the opening doors and all that. I just wish I'd get some kind of hint he's into me."

"Adam *does* like you," I say. "A guy doesn't take you out on a date if he doesn't. I saw how he acted at the river too. He seems into you."

"He's premed," she says abruptly. "I have to be smart around him."

"You are smart," I point out. "You would've had a perfect four point oh if not for PE."

"I know, and we have all these great conversations!"

I laugh, reaching for a napkin and wiping the excess glue from my fingertips. "I don't think you're confused," I say.

"I'm not?"

"No. I think you're scared."

Bailey reaches for the scissors, then grabs a piece of fragile tissue paper, staring at it. "I am."

"You're such a pain," I say, trying not to enjoy the feeling of having the tables turned. "You've convinced me all year that I'm dumb for being stuck on Landon, and you're totally hung up on a guy you just met, like, a month ago."

"Yeah, yeah," she says, finally slipping the scissors onto her fingers. "Just make sure you punch me if I start sounding like an idiot, okay?"

I punch her in the arm. "That won't be a problem."

She laughs as she cuts into the tissue paper. "Speaking of idiots, you and Landon seem to be getting cozier," she says.

"Landon is not an idiot."

"I was talking about you," she says, completing her cut and setting the scissors down.

"Hey!"

"I mean that with all the love in the world, of course." She reaches for a little Popsicle-stick structure, one we completed an hour ago and whose glue is completely set. "But you have to remember what I said. He's not boyfriend material. He's going to hurt you if you don't get over the idea of you two getting together for real."

"I know," I say, pinching two sticks together and then holding them still for the required time it takes to set. "It's, like, my brain is *screaming* to stop enjoying the time I spend with him, but I can't help it. When we're together, no matter what I tell myself, I still want to have this stupid happily ever after."

"That doesn't exist," she says.

"It could."

"If it could exist for you two, he would have picked you last year. You'd still be together. But he decided he found something better. When we're here at the ranch, you guys get thrown together a lot, and he figures he'll have fun for the summer. But he doesn't see you the way you see him."

"He could've changed," I say. I stare down at where my fingers are pinching the Popsicle sticks, watching as a drop of glue squeezes out from between them and drops onto the newspapers we've spread out on the ground.

"Let's go along with this delusional scenario and say he *has* changed. That he has genuine feelings and wants to live happily ever after with you. What happens in a couple of weeks when you're all, *Surprise! We broke up a year ago! I've been lying all summer!*"

"I don't know," I admit. "I haven't gotten that far."

"It's just . . . I'm worried about you, is all. You guys are hugging and kissing and laughing right now, but he's still the same guy who destroyed you last year. I don't want to pick you up off the floor again."

"I know," I say glumly. She's right. I'm getting too swept up in this. I need to hold back somehow. I sigh, setting down my lantern. "Do you want to take a break? I think the glue fumes are getting to me."

"It's Elmer's," she says.

"So?" I say. "I still feel like I need air."

She shrugs. "Yeah, sure, I guess I could use something to drink."

We stand, and I stretch out, arching my back like a cat. Sitting on the wooden floor for five hours has done me no favors.

Bailey puts the cap on her glue, and then we step back into the sunshine.

"Holy crap, it's roasting out here," I say as we step onto the pathways leading to our cabin.

"We should go buy Popsicles later. Grape."

"That's very . . . specific."

"Shut up," she says, elbowing me.

Moments later, we're stepping onto our front porch, and I yank open the door, eager for a cold soda and our dinky little fan. Instead, I stop in my tracks. "Oh. My. God," I say, staring into our cabin, blinking several times to see if the image in front of me goes away.

Red Solo cups.

Thousands of red Solo cups, all half-filled with water.

They cover the floor so fully that I can't even see the hardwood. They're balanced on the armrests and cushions of the couch. The windowsills. The kitchen counter. The top of the fridge. The microwave. The stools. The end tables. Even the top of the half-open bathroom door.

"Holy crap," Bailey says, stepping up beside me. "How did he even do this in half a day?"

"I had help," a voice calls out.

I whirl around to find Landon sitting on the front porch two doors down, watching us. It's not his cabin, but an empty one.

I cross my arms. "From who, an entire troop of Boy Scouts?"

He grins, propping his feet up on the railing and taking another sip of what looks like sweet tea. "I would never reveal my accomplices," he says.

"Of course it's plural," Bailey mutters under her breath. "He probably had half the cowboys on this ranch filling Solo cups all morning. How did we not catch wind of this?"

I ignore Bailey's commentary and stare down Landon instead. "We'll get you back for this you know," I say.

Landon grins. "Aw, just look at your face; 'it's vacant, with a hint of sadness. Like a drunk who's lost a bet.'"

I drop my jaw. "*Shaun of the Dead* does not count as a classic horror movie. It's a satire at best. A total blight on zombie movies everywhere."

His grin just widens, so I shake my head and close our cabin door, not ready to deal with dumping out the water and stacking up thousands of cups. Landon is entirely too smug over there in the shade, enjoying his iced tea.

I stomp away, heading back to the cafeteria, Bailey on my heels.

"Is it wrong that I'm kind of impressed?" I ask, screwing my lips to the side. "I mean the mousetraps were awesome, on a purely physical level, but this is genius. It's going to take us hours to clean it up and it required no actual pain."

I never saw this side of him last year. Everything was so simple. So . . . beautifully easy. This year, though, is so entirely different in such an amazing way that it's hard to believe he's even the same guy.

But he *is* the same guy. *He is, he is, he is.*

And even if Bailey's wrong, and he decides he wants to be with me, how would he react once I told him I'd been lying all summer?

God, how would I ever get myself out of this mess in one piece?

"So maybe he outdid you this time," Bailey says. "But it's not over yet."

CHAPTER TWENTY-SIX

We ride through the gates just as the sun makes its appearance over the rolling foothills, an orange beacon to guide us on what will be a full day's ride. Unlike in the movies, there's no covered wagon carrying our meals, no rustic squeak of wheels or toothless man we'll call Cookie.

No, tonight a guy in a big SUV will arrive at our destination using the highway, and he'll bring along a full-sized barbeque. So we're not slowed down by a wagon, instead it's the portly guy in a brand-new cowboy hat, holding on to the reins so tightly his horse keeps stopping and backing up.

I shift my weight and Zoey slows, moves out of the group of ranch hands and guests leaving the campus behind as we head toward the hills.

"I got it," I call to Landon, peeling away from him and trotting back to the rider, passing the dozen guests who are joining us. All in all, there are eighteen sets of hooves kicking up dust—in addition to the twelve guests, there are six staff members: me, Landon, and four longtime, year-round ranch hands. We're the six who will actually control the flow of the cattle. The other twelve are more like extras on a movie set, here to experience a dying tradition.

I reach the greenhorn and ride up alongside him, then pull to a stop like he has, watching as his horse tosses his head in frustration, annoyed to be held back when the rest of the group is walking casually ahead.

"Your reins should have slack in them," I say, demonstrating by wiggling my reins, showing him how loose they are. The man darts a look at me but doesn't loosen his grip. Instead his knuckles turn even whiter. "You can trust me. Zeke has done this ride a hundred times, and he's our most reliable horse. I promise that if you let go, he's not going to take off."

The guy rakes in a shaky breath, looking at me long enough that I can see the apprehension in his eyes. I keep talking in a low, even voice, like he's a cornered animal. "He's not a leader, just a follower. He will only go the speed of the rest of the horses, which is going to be a walk. All you have to do is sit up there and relax, and he'll autopilot you the whole way there, okay?"

His shoulders relax as he loosens the reins.

"It's okay to hold on to the horn until you get comfortable. After an hour or so you'll be totally relaxed. I swear."

He nods, smiling the slightest bit, and reaches for the horn.

His horse picks up an easy walk, and in a few minutes we've caught up to the back of the group. I walk next to him for a few more minutes, until I'm sure he's okay, and then I pull away and pick up a trot, swinging wide around the group and checking to be sure the other riders are doing okay. Just as expected, the horses are plodding quietly along, occasionally snorting or tossing their heads. They're all happy to be out of the arena and on the trails, but they're just as well behaved as always. These dozen horses have been ranch horses their whole lives and would never spook, even if a snake jumped right out at them.

I meet back up with Landon, who is at the front of the "herd," his often hyper horse just as relaxed as the others, and slow to a walk.

He smiles from beneath the brim of his cowboy hat, his eyes dark and sexy, his body swaying with the walk of his horse, his shoulders squared and strong yet his hands light on the reins.

He has never looked this good. This in control of his domain. I want to hate him for it, but part of me thinks this is the only time he's truly honest—with me, with himself. Not in a romantic sense. Not in a career sense. In that core way that matters. Deep inside, when all the BS slides away and you know what someone is made of.

It's out here on the trail where sometimes I think I see deep inside his soul, those moments he's utterly content, and somehow I finally *get* him. It doesn't mean we're meant to be, doesn't mean he won't break my heart.

It just means deep in his heart, he's something different. The guy who would gallop to the edge of a cliff to save you, in a dramatic scene like in *City Slickers*. He'd share his last drop of water with you, or if your horse went lame, he'd offer you his own and then walk, even if his boots made his feet blister and the sun dang near killed him.

He might still dump you for another girl, but out here, under the never-ending sky, he's mine. The guy I fall for over and over and over again.

"All good?" he asks.

"Yep. Just a little nervous." I glance back at the rider again, and he's already relaxing into the lull of his horse's easy walk. "He'll be fine in an hour or so."

"He probably should not have declined the pre-roundup lesson yesterday."

"Seems like it," I agree, nodding. "He'll probably be bowlegged by this time tomorrow."

Silence falls over us, and I'm content, listening to the gentle thud of hoofbeats, the occasional snort of a horse, or the jingle of a buckle as a horse tosses its head. I'm lost in a place a century or two ago, where cars and lockers and cell phones don't exist, and life was simple. "Can I ask you a question?" he says, a moment later.

"Shoot."

"If you could have *any* superpower, what would it be?" I glance up, surprised by how utterly left field his question is, but his expression is neutral, calm. He legit wants to know my dream superpower.

"There's only one right answer to this, isn't there?" I ask.

"Obviously."

I watch Zoey's ears swivel back and forth, trying to figure out which power Landon would choose. "Invisibility," I say.

"Now *that* is lame!" he says. "How can you pick that over flying?"

"Because anyone with a few hundred bucks and a passport

can fly. If I were invisible, I could watch people when they think they're alone."

"Well that's not creepy."

"I don't mean it like that. I just mean, everyone has a public self. A way they behave because they think they have to or because they want you to think they are a certain kind of person. But if I were invisible, I could see who they really are when they're alone, and their defenses are down."

"You say that like you've met some two-faced people."

"I don't know. Not necessarily two-faced, but maybe I'm just bad at reading them," I say. "At seeing beyond what they present to me. Maybe if I could be invisible, I'd understand them better. See them in their native environment or whatever."

He furrows his brow, unconvinced. "Still not better than flying."

"Guarantee, once you fly for a few weeks you'd be totally over it."

"There's no way *flying* would get old."

"All it does is get you from point A to point B. There are way too many options for alternative transportation. You can't waste your *one* opportunity for a superpower on *flying*."

"Not true. Can you imagine the things you could do? Good or bad. Rob banks or save people from burning buildings. Unlimited options."

"But with invisibility, you could still rob the banks, and they wouldn't even have a description of you. And you could go to any concert you want without tickets. You could go to movie sets and watch them film. You could stay in five-star resorts and no one would even know."

"Hmm . . . I can see how that would be nice. . . ." he says, screwing his lips up to the side, his eyes narrowed. "I mean, I've always wanted to hike up to the Hollywood sign, but it's got, like, thirty bazillion cameras and No Trespassing signs. They treat that place like Fort Knox. Even if I flew up there, I'd probably end up in handcuffs."

"No *way*," I say, incredulous.

"What?"

"Did I really just *convince* you of something?"

"Hey, I didn't say it was better than flying," he says, like he just realized I swayed his opinion. "Just that it had its merits."

"That's good enough for me," I say gleefully. "I practically won a debate with you."

He just shakes his head, and our conversation falls away as we continue to plod along, the horses in front of us kicking up dust. He reaches forward and pats Storm on the shoulder. "You know, it must have been weird, to do this for real."

"Yeah. I mean, sometimes out here, it really is real. We are actually moving the cows."

"But we don't have to. Or at least not like this," he says, motioning behind us to the tourists. The ones out here for the experience and not a purpose.

"What you really mean is it must have been weird to live then. When this was an actual way of life, and there were no . . . guests involved."

"Exactly."

I take in the desert landscape, the rolling hills, the chatter behind us. The sun beats down, and already I'm sweating, and the day's hardly begun. The comforts of my bed, a hot shower—they all fall away behind us. And yet, there's this inexplicable pull forward, to the draw of a hot meal tonight, followed by a long dip in the cool river, where an honest day's grime rinses away, and we feel new again. "I'm sure it was hard, but it was probably pretty amazing. To live this way."

He nods. I reach over and poke him. "It would have suited you. I bet you could've handled it."

"I'm sure you could've too," he says.

"Nah," I reply, grinning at him. "I don't think they would appreciate my freakish stylings."

"You're not a freak," he says, like the suggestion is idiotic.

I don't say it was *him* who nearly called me a freak several weeks ago, that first day we talked again. I don't know why he's denying he thinks I look like a freak now—if he doesn't think that way anymore, or if he's faking that he likes it.

I don't know how he feels about anything, anymore. I used to think I did. I used to think I had him figured out.

"Are you looking forward to the dance?" I ask.

"Sure. It sounds like it will be fun."

"Can you dance?" I know the answer. We danced together last year, and then I watched him at homecoming with Natalie. Before I heard about her dating that other guy.

"Yeah, my mom used to make me go to these swing dance lessons with her because there were always more girls than guys. I was, like, twelve, so I didn't realize how uncool that made me."

That explains why he was so good at the country-style dances last year. I picture twelve-year-old Landon dancing with his mom, and it fits. It also matches up with what he's said about stepping in for his dad.

I don't understand how, if he's such a good person, he let me fall for him and then walked away. I should stop searching for the answer, because clearly there is none.

I'll never again make fun of those dumb girls on *The Bachelor* who get dumped in favor of someone else and want the bachelor to give them a reason, like he's going to be all, "Oh, it was because you had spinach stuck in your teeth, and also you have a really annoying laugh."

But there's never really a reason he can give them. The fact of it is that he just loves someone else more. And last year, that someone else was Natalie.

But this year, it wasn't supposed to matter. I was supposed to be over him.

But now it *does* matter.

And that can't be good.

CHAPTER TWENTY-SEVEN

Two hours before dusk, we find the cattle milling about in a small valley tucked near the Columbia River. There are only two dozen of them—the ranch no longer makes a living on the cattle, so they only keep enough around to maintain the façade.

"You seemed rather deep in thought this afternoon," Landon says as we approach where we'll camp tonight.

"Yeah. It's quiet out here. Makes it easy to think."

"About?"

"You," I say, before I can stop myself.

"I *am* pretty amazing," he says.

I roll my eyes. "I know, right? Truly one of a kind."

"But no, seriously, what about me?"

"A lot of things," I say. "Like what's going to happen next week when our stay here is over and we . . . ." I pause, catching myself before I say *leave for college.* "We go back to Enum-claw."

"What do you mean, what's going to happen?"

I purse my lips for a second, telling myself not to go down this path, but I can't help it. "Are we going to be together?"

I want him to tell me of course we're going to be together, forever and ever. I want to hold on to this fantasy that he's falling for me this time around, that he finally sees me as that girl he can live happily ever after with, that there's no thoughts of Natalie in his head, no idea that he intends to kiss her and leave me behind.

And if that's true, if he wants to be with me, I'll find some way to make it work, make him understand why I had to lie to him all these weeks.

"Why wouldn't we be?" He looks so genuinely surprised, my heart does a little pitter-patter.

"I don't know. I don't know what I am to you. If this is a summer thing."

"I sure hope it's not just a summer thing," he says, adjusting his reins so that he can loop them around the horn. His free hand rests on the saddle pad, just behind his leg.

But why is this summer different, to him?

"I don't know. We haven't talked much about what happens in September."

"Don't you want to stay together?" he asks. Either I'm horrible at reading him, or he means it.

"Yes," I finally answer. "I want to stay together in September. And October and November and December."

As the words pour out, I know they're true. I want to be with him. I want to know what we could be.

"I believe you, so why do I feel like you don't believe *me*?"

We're approaching the group now, and it's time to help them dismount and untack and set up camp. "Can we finish this conversation later?" I ask.

"Yes. Because I feel like there's something you're not telling me."

Sometime after dusk, I get up from my seat on a folding camping chair, tossing my paper plate into the fire. I stand still, watching as the edges turn black and it slowly curls, then disappears into the ashes.

Landon stands, his presence heavy beside me, filling the air with anticipation. We haven't finished our conversation yet, and I know he's been confused all evening about my questions, my concern. And now I don't know what to tell him. Don't know how to say that I fully expect to be dumped in a week—if I didn't beat him to it—and what does he have to say for himself?

That would be stupid.

All around us, the guests are getting their bedding set up in their tents, some of them disappearing already, too sore from the day-long ride to hang out. Some of the others are forming mini-groups, enjoying the beverages and treats supplied by the ranch's SUV. It sits at the edge of camp, the windows rolled down and the radio humming with a quiet country song that floats out with the summer breeze.

"Where do you want to crash?" Landon asks, staring into the flames.

"That way, I guess," I say, pointing into the darkness, to where a log is vaguely visible on the ground, a natural barrier between what will become our bedroom for the night and the herd of horses and cattle that mill about.

Before I can respond, he reaches out and interlaces his fingers with mine, pulling me away from the other campers and toward a darkened corner of the camp, far from the heat of the fire and the light of the lanterns hanging from scrawny little trees. We walk in silence as the sounds of the group die out behind us and the chirps of crickets fill in the blanks. Above us, the stars twinkle, a never-ending blanket that seems so much more vivid than back at home. Those first few nights at the ranch last year, I couldn't stop staring at them, stop trying to count them all. I gave up at 842, when my eyes got heavy.

Landon stops by where we've laid out our tack and saddlebags, dropping my hand so that he can untie our bedrolls from the back of the saddle, and then he carries them both toward our destination. There, I spread out a thin outdoor blanket intended to keep our stuff clean. I purse my lips to keep from grinning as I unroll my sleeping bag, and Landon unties his own.

And then he goes to unroll it.

And it only unrolls halfway before it stops abruptly.

He tips his head to the side, his jaw drops, and I burst out laughing.

"You cut off the end of my sleeping bag!"

I laugh harder, and he playfully grabs me around the waist, picking me up and spinning me around before dropping me back onto the ground. "What am I going to do with you?" He doesn't let go of my waist, and so we're standing like that, me in his arms, blinking innocently up at him.

"I don't know," I say.

" 'I'll have an answer, or I'll have blood!' " he says, punching his fist into the night sky in an over-the-top sort of way.

"*Straw Dogs*," I say. "And fine, we can unzip my bag and lay on it. It's warm enough tonight."

"Deal." He reaches down and unzips my bag, spreading it out on the ground, then tossing our pillows on top. And then like that, we're done, and I'm staring at where we'll sleep, side by side, with only the stars as a blanket.

It's darker over here, private somehow even though I can see the dancing flames in the distance, can still occasionally hear a giggle or a shout.

I sit on the log, next to Landon, as we pull our boots and socks off. I put on a clean pair of socks and then reach into my bag to pull out my pj's—an oversized T-shirt with a big cherry on the front and matching cotton shorts. I glance at him and then back to our makeshift bed. Last year I'd slid into my bag and changed inside it, struggling to put it on without him seeing too much.

Landon sees my pause. "I'll turn around," he says, and then spins around so his back is to me.

"No peeking?" I ask. I don't know why I'm playing this game—he saw me in my bra and underwear when we went swimming at the start of the summer, then again in Bailey's little string bikini. But this feels different. Personal. Probably because we're about to sleep next to each other.

"Promise," he says, his voice sounding just a little huskier. "Unless you're plotting to steal all my clothes and run again."

I chuckle softly to myself as I stand on top of my sleeping bag.

"I had to cover myself with two palm fronds and run all the way to my cabin, you know."

"Sounds very Tarzan," I say as I swap my too-warm dirty button-up with the T-shirt, then shimmy out of my jeans and into the airy, comfortable shorts. "Done," I say, and he's spinning around on the log, then standing up. His eyes bore into mine with such intensity, I'm lost in his gaze. Until I realize that while he's staring at me, he's unbuttoning his pants. I jerk in an almost theatrical way and whirl around.

"Aw, modest?" he asks, chuckling under his breath.

"Just trying to return the favor," I reply.

I count to thirty before glancing back at him. He's in his boxers, shirtless, as he threads his arms through a clean T-shirt. When he pulls it over his head, his chest and abs tighten, completely drool-worthy.

I clear my throat and walk to my sleeping bag, busying myself with fluffing my pillow up so he won't notice how awkward I'm acting, all herky-jerky, like I can't remember how to work my arms, let alone breathe. I lie back and then he's beside me, and we're staring up at the sky, completely invisible to the group a couple hundred yards away.

For a moment, I let myself believe we're the only two people left on earth, and there was never Natalie, and there will be no other girl at WSU for him to choose this fall.

It's just me and him and the stars.

"I think this is my favorite place in the world," he finally says.

I nod. "It's breathtaking."

"I think no matter how old I get or where I am, this is one of those nights that just . . . imprints on you. Stays a vivid memory even a decade or two later, you know?"

I do know. Because he might not remember this from last year but I do, and I still remember every twinkling star, every snort of the nearby horses, every time his hand found mine and squeezed. Still remember how tired I'd been that next morning after spending almost an entire night listening to him breathe.

"Yeah. I know *exactly* what you mean," I finally say quietly.

"Where do you think you'll be?"

"When?"

"When you're remembering tonight," he says. "In a week, a month, a year. Are you applying anywhere?"

"UW and WSU. I want to stay in-state."

I don't tell him I've already accepted entrance to WSU, in Pullman. A few hours east of here, putting even more distance between me and my hometown. Classes start in a few weeks. I have my dorm assignment and meal card and everything.

"You?" I ask.

"I don't know yet."

But he does know. He's going to WSU, like me. He wore WSU T-shirts to school last spring, and at graduation, it was in the little program.

"You have time," I say, knowing he doesn't.

"Mm-hmm . . ." His hand finds mine in the darkness, and he squeezes it. "Why didn't we ever talk at school?" he asks. For a heartbeat I think he means after he chose her, and my mind races, spins into a million different responses. But then he says, "Why didn't you ever notice me like I noticed you?"

As I take in the calm, curious expression he's giving me, I realize he really wants to know.

"I don't know," I say honestly. "I mean, it's just like you said—we never had any classes together. You ran with your own crowd—Trevor and Rick and Nat—" I stop too late, realizing I don't want to say her name in front of him.

"Natalie," he says. And hearing the way he says her name, like it means something, sends a stab to my heart. Even as we're still holding hands, there's something about her that draws him in, some quality to her I know I'll never encompass. Some-how she's both popular and respected, ethereal and a party girl, sweet yet strong. A thousand contradictions all rolled into one amazing person.

"Yeah. She was . . . she was who I was thinking of earlier. When I was asking you about September and beyond. You guys were so close before this summer. I guess I was worried . . ."

"That I'd go back to her?" he asks, surprise and confusion evident in his voice. But that doesn't make sense, because he does go back to her. The idea of reuniting with Little Miss Perfect shouldn't inspire surprise.

"Uh-huh. I was thinking that life on this ranch feels differ-ent than the real world. *I* feel different. And maybe when we left, you'd become someone else. You'd get together with her and leave me behind," I say, and the honesty is freeing.

"Well, I mean, she's . . . a really amazing girl," he says. I wait for him to say something else, but he doesn't, and I'm desperate for him to speak again. He's supposed to assuage my fears. Supposed to laugh at the idea he'd get back with her.

"What happened?" I ask. "You guys seemed really into each other last spring."

"We broke up," he says simply. I believed that, last year. But I saw how quickly they picked right back up when he returned, and I know it's not quite true, that it's somewhere in the shades of gray, that all summer long he was harboring feelings for her. Maybe when he was with me, it was really just me, but the moments were fleeting. He'd been with her, in so many ways.

"Why? Did you not love her?"

"Of course I did."

The silence stretches on and on. I hate that he's not filling in the blanks. I gaze up at the stars, my mouth dry. My stomach hurts at his admission. He's supposed to love me, not her.

"So, she dumped you?" I ask, finally, desperate for an answer, confused as to why he doesn't feel the need to reassure me if he really thinks we're together. Why would a guy tell his girlfriend stuff like this?

Maybe I'd never really understand Landon, not even after *two* summers.

"Yes. I mean, that wasn't our problem, exactly. . . ."

"But that's how it went. She dumped you."

He screws his lips up to the side a little, then nods. "It was her idea, yeah. But it was for the best."

So she broke up with him but he loved her. And at the end of the summer, when she decided it was a mistake, he was all too happy to take her back. I swallow and stare up at the stars, wishing they gave me the same peace as they had moments ago, but somehow they seem to just be spotlighting the hurt that will no doubt be coming in a week's time.

"Hey," he says, and I meet his eyes. "Don't look so . . ."

"Hurt?" I ask.

"Yeah. It's over. I've moved on."

"I'm fine," I say, knowing I'm not.

"You really are amazing, you know that? So different from her."

"How so?" I ask, suddenly needing to know.

"She's just . . . very sweet. Kind of a pushover. I mean I can't even convince you that Sean Connery is the ultimate James Bond. . . ."

I smile and shove his shoulder. I can't believe that I spent all of last summer letting him win arguments because I thought he wouldn't like me otherwise. That's so not me.

"I don't know. In some ways, it's almost like she's too perfect. She didn't fire me up like you do. There's sparks with us, you know?"

"I see," I say, because what else is there to respond with?

"Why do I feel like I'm screwing this up?"

I shrug, but I don't comment because there are too many thoughts battling for attention in my head. Who she is, who I am. Who she was, who I was then. And whether there's a difference at all, or if I'm the same naïve girl a second time.

What's that saying?

Fool me once, shame on you.

Fool me twice . . .

I frown. Beside me, Landon shifts his weight so that he's lying on his side. He reaches over, touches my face, rubbing soft little circles on my cheek, and I close my eyes, memorizing the feeling.

"Mack, what I'm trying to tell you . . ." His voice trails off, and I open my eyes again, realizing that for the first time in the years I've known him, he looks edgy, nervous. He meets my gaze. "What I'm trying to say is that I loved her. She's a wonderful person. But I'm *in* love with you."

Emotions roar to life in my throat, and a boulder lodges itself there until it's hard to breathe. I want to cry, because I don't know if I believe him and that's what hurts most.

I love him back, but I don't trust him.

He didn't say "I love you" last year. Because he *didn't* love me. I fell so hard, but he didn't love me back. So what have I done so differently this time to change things? Or is it an act, and the rug will be pulled out from under me just like before?

I blink the tears that brim, hoping he can't see them in the darkness. But I fail, because the thumb tracing circles on my cheek slides over, brushing a tear off my lashes.

Landon might remember the stars most, but me, it's the heat of his skin and the breathless anticipation as his lips touch mine, soft, gentle, his tongue tracing the edge of my lips.

Any remaining sounds of the night disappear as I slip my arm around him, welcoming the weight against me as he leans across me, deepening our kiss, wanting desperately to forget every complication our relationship has.

The moment seems to stretch on as long as the night sky,

enveloped by the darkness. And then too soon he pulls away, rolling onto his back and staring up at the stars.

"Good night, Mackenzie," he says, a husky whisper in the moonlight.

"Good night," I say, knowing tonight will be just like the one last year.

I'm going to spend all of it just listening to him breathe.

CHAPTER TWENTY-EIGHT

"I think I might actually like that more than the blue dress," Bailey says from her position in our tiny bathroom. I can't see her, but every now and then I hear the hair spray bottle. She must be wearing a whole gallon of it by now.

She did mine first. It's piled on my head in pretty little ringlets, pinned and tucked. One dangles down in front of my eye, but I've sworn to Queen Bailey that I won't touch it. She even used a half-dozen bobby pins that have pretty little crystals on the end, so that every time I turn one of them catches the light, and a glitter of sunshine dapples the wall inside our cabin.

"Yeah," I say. "The blue dress just wasn't punk rock enough." Bailey snorts and I grin. "I'm kidding."

I click the heels of my cowboy boots together like I'm Dorothy and I just want to go home. But I'd never go home, not tonight. Not with the hours of fun stretching before us. Not with knowing how little time I have left with Landon before he finds out what I've been up to all summer.

I'm sinking into the old couch in our cabin a little at a time, so I sit up more, smoothing out the multicolored tulle skirt. The layers are super short and they puff out at weird angles, and I was worried I'd end up showing off my underwear, so I found totally cute white lace tights to wear underneath them. I'm in love with the whole outfit, and Bailey whistled when she saw it all put together.

"You really do look hot. Landon is going to fall all over himself when he sees you."

I frown, staring down at my pink polished nails, another product of the Bailey-driven makeover. I reach over and grab the Sharpie sitting discarded on the table next to me, then add a black star to each nail. "Yeah, about that," I admit.

She's quiet for a second, and then she steps into our room. "What about it?"

She's staring at me like she's worried. "So, um, I kinda didn't tell you *everything* about the cattle drive. . . ." I take a deep breath. "He told me he loved me."

She looks at me like I just grew a unicorn horn out of my forehead. "You believe him, don't you? You want happily ever after."

"I don't know what to think. He didn't say it last year. So now I don't know if he really fell this time, if it all worked out as planned, or if he's just playing a better game." I shrink back into the couch.

"Oh my God, you fell in love with him all over again, didn't you?"

"No," I say honestly.

"Good," she says, reaching up to feel how hot her hair is where it's spun around the curling iron. She steps toward the bathroom just as I speak again.

"Because I never fell out of love with him to begin with."

She freezes and the silence is heavy, thick with what I've said.

"You have to dump him," she says, almost accusingly. "Promise me you're still dumping him tonight."

I shake my head. "I can't. Not if he's willing to give us a chance. I want it all, Bailey. I want to tell him the truth and I want him to tell me it's okay, and I want to go to WSU as a couple. I want to cram for tests and stay up late eating pizza. I want to be with him. Away from this ranch."

"Oh, Mack," she says, sighing as she turns around and steps back into the bathroom. "You are so screwed."

CHAPTER TWENTY-NINE

By the time Bailey and I make it to the big dining hall where the dance is held, the music is vibrating the pathways, and the noises of the crowd are almost as loud. Whistling, boot stomping, clapping . . .

An overwhelming sense of déjà vu sweeps over me, and despite the warmth of the late August night, I get goose bumps. Suddenly it's me in a pair of tight-fitting jeans with a long, flowing white peasant blouse as I make this same walk, eager to see Landon. Eager to know what would happen next.

Bailey bumps my hip, and I'm brought back to the present.

The dance is my favorite part of the summer. For one night, and one night only, the ranch hands and the guests, the maids and the managers, all get together for one big blowout. We get away with comingling because they talk up the night like crazy, hyping it up how there's this big, two-hundred-year-old tradition of the ranch owners throwing a shindig for the ranch hands at the end of a successful cattle drive. A celebration for everyone, no matter how old or young, rich or poor you are. So even the richest of the rich guests don't mind mingling with the staff. Drinking with the staff. Dancing with the staff.

Bailey and I step up onto the wide porch, and I glance at the couple on an enormous swing at the far end, in the shadows, wondering if they came together or if they're simply leaving together. Tonight has a way of running away with people.

Back in the day, the rancher would open his pockets and "profit share," as it were, after such a great season. That's what the brochures say, anyway. The profits don't come from the cattle anymore.

The guests are really paying for it anyway. This weekend boasts the second-highest rental fees, after the Fourth of July.

The place is transformed from the big guests-only dining hall—the round tables Bailey and I helped clear giving way to an expansive dance floor. Above them dangle the paper lamps Bailey and I spent hours assembling—they hang from every conceivable spot, giving the room a warm, mellow glow.

"Wow. Our little arts-and-crafts project turned out pretty amazing," Bailey says, her words coming out breathy. A DJ is set up in the corner, so tucked away one would think the music was playing on its own. A few scattered tables remain, covered in western tablecloths, and they all have big mason jar candles on them.

"Man, I love this stupid hick dance," Bailey says. "It's way better than homecoming."

We grin at each other. I couldn't agree more. "Is Adam here?"

She shrugs, suddenly looking nervous as her eyes dart around. "I don't know. He said dances aren't his thing, but that I should have fun."

I frown. "There's no way you got that decked out to sit on the sidelines."

"But I don't think he's coming," she says.

"He'll show up."

Bailey looks down for a second, pretending to scuff away a stain on the floor with the toe of her adorable little ankle boots.

"You're seriously into him, aren't you?"

She shrugs but doesn't deny it.

"Never thought I'd see the day," I say.

"It's not *that* crazy," she says.

"Right. Totally. Not at all surprising that you would get stuck on a boy. A handyman, at that."

"You say that like I'm a snob or something. And besides, the handyman thing is his summer job. College is expensive," she says, crossing her arms.

"It's rather convenient that you'll both be at UW in another couple of weeks," I say.

"I know, right? That's why I have to figure out if he's into me before then, when he'll be surrounded by all those smarty-pants sophomores and I'm just a freshman." She frowns. "I mean, I really, *really* like him. He's different." Her eyes roam the crowd, searching for him. I might break his kneecaps later if he doesn't show, because there's way too much hope in her eyes. If he breaks her heart, he's a dead man.

"Different how?"

"He calls me out when I'm trying too hard. I tried to play the Little-Miss-Innocent act and he laughed at me. Laughed! Like it was hilarious."

"Do I want to know what the Little-Miss-Innocent act is?"

"You know, like after a date, you invite them into your cabin for a movie, but you act like you're going to spend all night watching *Finding Nemo* and putting tiny little marshmallows in your hot chocolate or some crap. Then the guy inevitably makes a move, and you're obligated to act surprised before making out with him."

I snicker. "I feel like this conversation just took a left turn into a really warped Swiss Miss commercial."

"Oh, come on, you get what I mean. I invited him in for a movie, and he just stared at me, and I was, like, what, it's just a movie, and he laughed and was all *right . . .*" She's rattling off their conversation so fast it's hard to follow as she talks with her hands and rolls her eyes. "And then he didn't come in!"

I scrunch up my nose. "He said *no thank you*?"

"Yes!"

Her shock is amusing. "You know, he could just be taking things slow."

"If he doesn't want to make out," she says, sighing in exasperation, "how do I know if he likes me?"

I shake my head. "Well, considering he just walked in and is heading this way, and he supposedly hates dances, I'm guessing he really likes you."

She whirls around so abruptly she knocks into me, elbowing me straight in the stomach. "Ooof," I say, rubbing my belly.

Bailey can't take her eyes off Adam as he pushes through

the crowd. It takes only one glance at the way he's looking at her to know he's just as into her as she is into him. He doesn't even seem to notice me standing next to her, because his eyes are trained on hers. I'm not sure why Bailey hasn't figured out that whatever he feels, it's real, and it's just as strong as her own feelings.

"I'll catch up later," I murmur to Bailey, and pull away from her just as he gets there, and the two are grinning like fools at each other.

I slip into the crowd as the music kicks up a notch, from an easy line dance to a couples' dance. I thread my way between the ebb and flow of the dance floor, trying to get to the other side, where I can grab a soda and people watch, but I'm only halfway there when a hand finds mine.

I look up and Landon's staring down at me, his eyes dark, his hair pushed back off his forehead with gel or something. My mouth goes dry and I swallow hard, staying silent as he pulls me toward the middle of the floor, until we're standing under the swirling lights.

And then without warning, he spins me, and we're dancing, the beat of the song bleeding into the background as we find our own rhythm.

He leads, pushing and pulling until we're doing something vaguely resembling a swing dance, and I remember him talking about the lessons with his mom. He obviously hasn't forgotten a thing.

"You weren't lying when you said you could dance," I shout over the music as he turns with me, our bodies together then apart, together then apart.

"There's a lot about me you don't know," he says.

And for a second it reminds me of that first day in the river, before he fell from his horse, when all of his words seemed to have double meaning. But he's grinning, enjoying the dance, not thinking of regrets.

"Oh," I say.

"Don't worry, I've got all the time in the world to share my secrets," he says.

God I hope that's true. I hope we have so much more time to get to know each other. He pulls me to the side, guides my arm over my head, then lets go, and I'm sliding away before being twirled back at him, and then we're touching again, his hands on mine.

Around and around we go, until I'm breathless and the song transitions to a slower one, and he pulls me against him. I rest my head against his shoulder as we both breathe, in and out in time with a Taylor Swift song, one about losing and last kisses.

And the longer we sway, the longer he holds me against him, the longer I inhale the scent of soap and something else, something distinctly him, the more I hurt.

I've gone and done it.

I thought I loved him before, and I did, but this, what I feel now, it's all-consuming. Maybe it's because now I know what it's like to lose him. Maybe it's because things feel different this year. Less artificial, somehow, which seems so insanely stupid since it was supposed to be fake all along.

But the conversations we had, they dug deeper. Despite that I was supposed to pretend to be someone else . . . somehow I ended up showing him the real me. Those stupid pranks that had me laughing, horror movie quotes, those heated debates I discovered I actually *enjoyed*. . . . I can't not think we're perfect for each other.

And suddenly it's hard to breathe, and I can't dance with him for another second.

"You okay?" he asks, his voice low in my ear. I nod my head but don't speak. He rubs a soft circle on my lower back.

I don't think I have it in me anymore—the lying. I can't handle it.

"Do you think we can get out of here?" I ask, pulling away from him.

"Are you sure? You'll be all dressed up with no place to go. . . ."

"I'm sure. Let's go down to the swimming hole so we can talk. While everyone's here we'll have it to ourselves."

"Okay. Yeah," he says, eyeing me a little sideways. I didn't do this last year. Last year, we spent all night here, laughing and dancing until our feet hurt. He leads me off the floor, and near the exit, we see Bailey and Adam, both leaning against the wall, staring at each other. She's more beautiful than I've ever seen her. She beams whenever she's looking at him.

"We're heading out," I call to Bailey. Confusion crosses her face for a split second before she masks it.

"Um, okay, have fun?"

"Yeah, uh, see you at the cabin later," I call to Bailey, letting Landon pull me through the door.

We walk down the pathways, my despair growing, building, bubbling as my arms swing against my little tulle skirt. Even though the summer heat is still oppressive, I can't help but think about how in a few more weeks, the heat will break, fall will barrel in, and we'll all be gone.

Landon slings his arm around my shoulders, and I lean into him, breathing him in again. I need him close to me right now, because this could be the last time he wants to speak to me.

I'm telling him the truth. And when I do, he's going to run from me, just like he did last time, but I can't not tell him what I feel.

And so I want this last touch, his skin hot on mine, before I ruin us.

We get to the river, and I kick off my shoes, glancing back at Landon before stepping into the water, ankle-deep.

"You're going to wreck your dress," he calls out as he slips his T-shirt over his shoulders, the moonlight catching the contours of his muscles.

I'm going to wreck so much more than this dress. But instead I say aloud, "I know."

I step deeper into the water, until the river reaches the hem of my skirt, and it flares out farther, floating up around me. The water is cool against my skin, but I feel hot, dizzy, out of touch. I don't want to do this. I don't want to say good-bye to him again.

I want to have forever.

I stand there in silence, staring out at the water, in so much pain it's hard to speak. Then I turn back and wade until the water is a little more shallow, and I sit down in the water, near the banks, so that the cool liquid swirls around my hips and waist, but so I can pull my legs up close to me, hugging my knees to my chest. He finishes stripping off his jeans, and then he sits down next to me, his legs stretched out in front of him. Under the water, he finds a rock and lifts his hand to toss it across the river. The *plunk* is loud in the darkness.

I grind my teeth, trying to figure out the exact way to do this. How can I say these words when they're lodged firmly in my throat?

He scoots over, so we're close, hip to hip, side to side.

"I have to tell you something," I say, my voice coming as a whisper in the night.

"Okay."

I take in a ragged breath. "I've been lying to you."

I can nearly hear the sounds of my words falling around us, like rocks breaking the surface of the river.

"About?" His hand finds my back, rubs up and down, up and down.

"Everything." I stare out at the water, at the places it ripples around the rocks and boulders. "When you hit your head . . . when you got that concussion . . . we weren't together. We broke up a year ago."

His hand stills, but he doesn't speak. All I can hear is my heart as it bangs painfully against my ribs. But then his hand slides off of my back, and I ache for the loss of his touch.

"You hurt me last year. Deeply. It took me weeks to pull myself together, and even then, I missed you. And I wanted you to feel that. So I manipulated you."

"I know."

The world goes silent as his words swirl just like the river water. And then all at once, the silence turns to roaring, like a freight train blasting through my ears.

He knows? How could he know?

"What? No."

"Yes."

"No," I say, unable to believe that he knew what I was doing.

"Yes," he repeats.

"How?" My chest heaves, and I wrap my arms more tightly around my legs. "When?"

"When did I remember that we'd broken up already?"

I purse my lips and nod.

"A month ago. Maybe a little longer. It didn't happen all at once. Bits and pieces sort of clicked into place. I was confused at first as to how we were together again when I remembered us being apart . . . but then I realized that meant even *you* knew we weren't together, but for some reason were acting like it."

"And you didn't say anything."

He doesn't respond, just watches the ripples of light dancing on the surface of the water. Why isn't he angry? He should be telling me off right now, infuriated. Yet he played along.

"No," he says, slowly.

"Why?"

I twist toward him, staring into the darkness of his eyes, and he finally meets my gaze. "Because it was the only way I could be with you."

I blink, stare, then blink and stare some more, somehow unable to move, to function, to create coherent thoughts. "You chose her. Why would you want to be with me now?" I snap my jaw shut because I have no right to be indignant, not when he knows I've spent almost two months playing an elaborate game with him.

"Look, let me explain it all, okay?"

I swallow down the emotions screaming in my throat.

"Last summer . . . was amazing. I was afraid to be with you at first, because I'd just broken up with Natalie, and . . . I don't know. I was confused. I'd been with her for three years and we were best friends, and I love her."

I feel a little stab to my heart.

"But I never really fell *in* love with her. The problem is, I didn't know it at the time."

His hand finds mine, where it sits against the muddy river-bank, and he covers it with his own, giving it a squeeze. "Me and Natalie, we grew up together, you know? She was the girl next door. My first kiss, my first girlfriend. She was the only thing I'd ever known, until you."

I wait for him to go on, because I don't know where he's going with this, and too many possibilities are spinning in front of me.

"When she broke it off . . . it destroyed me. I thought I'd lost everything."

I know exactly how he felt.

"She wanted to stay friends, and I guess I really clung to the idea that we'd somehow patch things up. That I could have my girlfriend back and my world back and everything would be perfect, like it had always been."

Underwater, his free hand finds a rock, and then he's skip-ping it across the river one, two, three times. We watch it dis-appear, watch the ripples spread across the water, before he speaks again.

"Sometimes things feel perfect because they're easy. No fric-tion. No fights. No *problems*. Last year, I guess I hadn't figured out there was a difference between that kind of perfection and being in love. So when she broke up with me, I didn't want to let go."

He frowns. "When I met you, I wasn't ready for another relationship, but I guess I sort of threw myself into one anyway. It just . . . it felt good, to be around you. To forget about her for a while, you know?"

"I was your rebound?" I ask, cringing.

"I know that sounds terrible. But you have to understand how long I'd been with her. Three years, we were dating. We'd been best friends before that. I just didn't know who I was without her."

"So you used me to get over her."

He sighs. "That's how it started out. You were my escape. A way to forget her."

I don't reply.

"You have to have noticed the difference this year. Last time around, I was holding back. I wasn't ready to be with you. You were the right person at the wrong time."

"I would've understood, if you needed to take it slow. You could've told me you weren't over her," I say, my voice cracking.

"I couldn't, though. It was hard enough to admit it to myself."

"But I would've understood. I would have gone slower if I'd known you weren't ready for a serious relationship. I mean, I told you I loved you," I accuse. "And you kissed me. You made me believe what we had was real."

"I know."

"Why?"

He worries his bottom lip. "Because . . . I don't know. At the end of the summer, I was just coming around again, looking forward instead of back. Thinking maybe you and me had a real chance, you know? And you'd started getting under my skin. You started making me think of things that had nothing to do with Natalie."

"Then what happened in September?"

"She called me two days before we left the ranch," he says. "She wanted to get back together. She told me she'd made a mistake."

"And you went running back to her."

He doesn't refute it. Doesn't even move. I fight the lump growing in my throat. Nothing he's saying changes anything. He picked her. She won, I lost.

"I was a fool," he says, when he finally breaks the silence. "I found it impossible to choose, and by default, that meant hurting you. But the way it felt to lose her was nothing compared to you. And this time it was my own fault. I should have realized how much I cared about you."

"You're still the one who made the choice. You kissed her. You knew I'd find out."

"I know. But I didn't realize it until it was too late. I went back to what was familiar, instead of what was right. You. Us. We were always right, when we were together. I was just too stupid to see it."

He stares into my eyes with such intensity that I believe he regrets the decision. I just don't know if it matters. "I broke up with her three weeks later."

That's not possible. They were together until spring, when she got with the guy from White River. Even at graduation, I saw them, leaning against each other, laughing. "But you went to homecoming. You still ate lunch together every day. You were a couple all year."

He shook his head. "No. I told you, we were best friends. Of course we still hung out. But when we broke up the second time . . . I don't know. We both just let it go, you know? Any idea of a romance between us. Sometimes you want to hang on tighter to something that's familiar, even when it's not right. We were both just so relieved to admit that we did love each other, but not in that way, you know? But it took meeting you . . . and then losing you . . . to understand what *perfect* actually was."

He shuts his eyes before looking at me again. "And then you come back around this year, with your pranks and your insane hair and your fiery attitude, and I fell for you a thousand times harder."

I'm shaking my head, blinking away the tears that threaten to spill. "Why didn't you tell me when you realized you'd made a mistake? That it was me you wanted?"

"Because I didn't deserve you. What I did to you, dumping you at a moment's notice and choosing her, it wasn't right." He sighs so hard it's like he shrinks. "It made me like my dad. You trusted me, believed in me, and I left you behind. Everything I had ever avoided being, and in one choice, I became him."

He rubs his eyes. "Maybe I should've gone to you and begged for your forgiveness. I just couldn't imagine you giving it to me. Someone like Natalie, sure. She's sweet and forgiving and . . . soft. But you, you're different. You expected loyalty and I ran. Just like him. You deserved better, and I figured you knew it."

"I don't know what to say." I smile sadly as tears make

everything shimmer. It's the strangest mix of happiness and regret.

"I still don't remember much of what happened between my accident and the Fourth of July. It started coming together around then, when I saw you run the arena with the flag. I knew I'd seen that before. And then I talked to my mom a few days later, and she gave me this weird recap of your conversation with her. It all started to clarify."

"And yet, you didn't put a stop to my little plan."

He nods. "Yeah. I mean, the thing is, I didn't know what you were up to, but I figured I could do this one thing for you. Give you this summer, for whatever reason you wanted it. I owed you that much."

I shook my head. "I wanted to hurt you so badly. You have no idea."

" 'We all go a little mad sometimes,' " he says.

I smile through my tears. "*Psycho*. But I wasn't just mad. I was so hurt by you that I wanted you to know how it felt. And so I wanted you to fall in love with me so I could dump you. Tonight."

"Oh."

I swallow around the lump in my throat. "I needed to hear you say you loved me, and then I was going to rip your heart out just like you did to me. Except I screwed it all up."

"How did you screw it up?"

"I fell for you even harder than I did before. I started seeing other sides of you, sides I didn't see last year. I started thinking you weren't such a bad guy after all."

We turn to one another, and he practically glimmers, dancing in the teardrops clouding my vision. He reaches out as the first one brims, wiping it away, cupping my cheek before pulling me closer.

"Don't cry," he whispers, and it only makes the tears fall harder, unstoppable. Our lips touch and I melt into him, pursing my lips against the hurt and the tears, and giving in to him, letting myself fall completely. Letting my fear wash away with the river. "Please don't cry."

I close my eyes and try to rein in the tears. "Do you think we could cancel the breakup?"

He pulls away but rests his forehead against mine and stares straight into my eyes. " 'There's nothing in the world I wouldn't give for that. Yes, I would give even my soul for it.' "

"*Dorian Gray,*" I whisper.

He nods. "Mack, even if you wanted to, I couldn't let you break up with me. I'm hopelessly, stupidly in love with you, and I don't think I can handle being apart again."

I think I'm laughing and crying at the same time, and I throw my arms around him, letting him pull me half into his lap, letting him rock me as I nestle into his neck.

"I love you too, Landon. I love you too."

CHAPTER THIRTY

I pull lightly on Zoey's reins, turning her toward a path I can barely see in the predawn light. Her shoes hit a few rocks, making a pleasant clinking noise as she navigates the trail. I rest my hand on her withers, trusting her eyesight more than my own as we hit the point that the path curves upward, and I have to lean forward to keep from sliding off her back.

Behind me, Landon's borrowed horse snorts, and I hear him pat the horse's neck, murmuring something under his breath. It's weird to see him on a horse other than Storm, but his gelding is miles away, in his paddock at home.

We're riding bareback, and Zoey's body heat is warming me though my jeans, the only thing keeping me from turning into a human Popsicle. I've never been to the ranch in December, and it's so cold that my breath is coming out in foggy clouds, and my fingers are turning stiff. I zip my jacket up all the way to my chin, then hunch my shoulders and lean into the cold breeze ruffling Zoey's mane.

"Brrrr," Landon says as if reading my mind.

" 'That cold ain't the weather,' " I say, loud enough for him to hear. " 'That's death approaching.' "

"Thirty Days of Night," he calls out.

The game I started at the ranch is now a full-blown war, with both of us working horror movie quotes into everyday conversation. Last week, I managed twenty-three lines in one day, breaking Landon's record of nineteen. I didn't get a trophy or anything, but Landon says he's still working on it.

Zoey picks her way over a rocky stretch of path, and then it opens up, and I pull back, letting Landon ride up alongside me.

"Yeah, next time we do this, I'm wearing gloves," I say, flexing my hand in and out, trying to force the blood back into my fingertips. "You could've warned me, you know."

"I've never done this in the winter," he says. "But it'll be worth it, I swear."

"I trust you," I say. And I do. In the four months since we left the ranch, he's proven I can. Proven he really loves me. We both go to WSU, and even though our dorms are a long, hilly walk apart, we make it every day. And yeah, he kind of ruins my study time, but I managed to survive my first semester all right, and now it's Christmas break. Two glorious weeks of no classes and plenty of Landon.

The ranch is halfway between WSU and our hometown of Enumclaw, Washington, which means it fit perfectly into our holiday plans. We dropped in yesterday, and Mr. Ramsey let us use one of the empty cabins for the night. This afternoon we'll get back to Enumclaw, and tomorrow we're meeting up with Bailey and Adam.

But now, it's six thirty in the morning and here we are, on horseback, picking our way up a trail in the dark. Because Landon insisted on it.

Zoey tosses her head, and the chain under her chin jingles into the silence, creating its own melody as we crest the edge of the hill.

"This way," Landon says, leading us to the left. Zoey follows automatically, so I barely touch the reins.

Landon is nothing but a dark shadow in front of me, an outline of broad shoulders and a knit hat, since he didn't bring his cowboy hat to college. It's been weird adjusting to him in ball caps and beanies.

"So, how's that invisibility working out for you?" Landon asks.

"It's great," I say, knowing where this conversation is leading. He's still never given up on the idea that flying has just as many, or more, uses than invisibility. He can't take that there was that one weak moment he practically admitted I was right.

"Just saying, if you'd gone with flying, we'd be at the top already."

"Yeah, and if you'd gone with invisibility, maybe you would've done better on the biology final."

"How is invisibility an asset in test taking?"

"We could've snuck into Professor Carter's house and peeked at the test."

"You're not convincing me. There are simply more uses for flying."

"If you say so," I say.

After a few more minutes of walking, he finally slows and then stops. I pull up too, so that our knees knock into each other.

"Why are we here again? You're being all mysterious."

"I thought you liked surprises," he teases.

"I like getting back to my dorm room and realizing you've left a box of chocolates on my bed. I like finding your notes in my pocket in the middle of calculus. I'm less a fan of freezing my butt off."

"Just give it another minute," he says.

I sigh and quit complaining, instead petting Zoey in circles as a way to warm my fingertips. She heaves her own big sigh, lowering her head a bit, relaxing.

I don't know when the shift occurs, because it's gradual, the edges of the sky warming, tinged with pink.

And then it happens: the barest sliver of sun appears, beams of warmth kissing the valley floor below us. We sit in silence as the sun dawns, rises above the rolling hill, and the sky becomes awash in yellows and pinks and blues, the few clouds appearing almost purple.

"It's . . . beautiful," I say, almost breathless. It's the prettiest sunrise I've ever seen. I forget how cold I am, that I can barely feel my nose or the tips of my ears, instead staring out at the horizon, soaking it in, memorizing the sight of it.

"I came up here after I got that call from Natalie last year," he says. I turn to him, but he's staring out at the sunrise. "The one where she asked me to take her back. She called at two a.m., and we talked for over an hour. That was the night I decided to give you up."

I tangle my fingers into Zoey's mane, studying the sun's ascent as I listen to Landon.

"I couldn't sleep and I felt stir-crazy, so I got Storm out and we walked aimlessly for a while before stumbling on this viewpoint just as the sun was rising."

"I'm glad you found it," I say. "It's something I'll never forget."

He finally looks at me. "Me either. I'm glad you're here. It makes everything we went through . . ." His voice trails off. "It makes it worth it."

I nod.

Natalie went to USC for college. Landon Skypes with her from WSU sometimes, and he introduced us. She actually had the nerve to apologize to me, once she found out about how everything went down between me and Landon. As much as I wanted to hate her once, I've realized that everyone makes mistakes.

Lucky for me, though, letting Landon go is one thing I'm never doing again.

My reverie is broken when Landon touches my knee, and I turn to him. He leans across the space between our horses, and my eyes slip closed just as his lips touch mine.

And as the sun rises over the desert, we kiss.

ACKNOWLEDGMENTS

Many thanks to:

My agent, Bob Diforio, who I am convinced never sleeps. You're a joy to work with and I appreciate all you do.

My editor, Caroline Abbey, who pushed me in all the right ways. I'm thrilled to be working with an editor as talented as you. Thank you, as well, to Laura Whitaker for your fresh eyes and smart questions.

My crit partner, Cyn Balog, for reading a very early version of this and waving the pom-poms.

My husband and daughter, for understanding what it means to be on deadline, and only bothering me when it's a gummy bear emergency.

Photo © Amber Sheree

Mandy Hubbard lives in Enumclaw, Washington, not far from the dairy where she grew up. Her first kiss was received on horseback. The love of horses lasted, but the boyfriend didn't. Now, she spends her time writing, running, and watching way too much MTV. She is also the author of *Prada & Prejudice* and *You Wish*. Follow her on Twitter, @MandyHubbard, or visit her website to learn more: www.MandyHubbard.com.

WANT MORE OF WHAT YOU CAN'T HAVE?

*Read on for a glimpse at another romance filled with
gelato, sightseeing, and off-limits amore!*

There's every color of gelato you can imagine. All the little flavor signs are in Italian, but I do recognize some of the words, like "nutella" and "amaretto." Each tub of gelato is its own work of art—a swirly mound drizzled with glistening sauce or sprinkled with nuts, chocolate bits, or fruit.

The sweaty crowd impatiently nudges me to move along, and a bored server waits for me to order. Feeling the pressure to make a fast decision, I point to the one called *stracciatella* because it looks the most like cookies and cream, then pick an unlabeled green one, hoping that it's mint and not something weird like pistachio.

As I walk out to find a place to sit, a family of three—speaking what I'm pretty sure is French—abandons their table, so I slip into one of the little chairs before anyone else claims it. I set my cup on the table and take aim with my camera, zooming in nice and close with a large aperture so everything but my focal point will be blurred together. *Snap.* My first photograph in Italy.

"Nice camera."

Startled, I glance up as a scruffy-faced guy about my age pulls out a chair across the table from me.

"Thanks."

"Mind if I sit here?"

I give a slight shake of my head, looking him up and down quickly. Aside from the insane amount of curly, dark hair on the top of his head, he sort of reminds me of Morgan's older brother. Tall, same toned build, super-light-brown eyes. The crush that crushed me.

He takes a bite of his gelato. "I'd never be able to use one of those big cameras. Too many buttons."

I can't help but smile. I haven't even been in Italy a whole day, but I'm already relieved to hear English—*my* English. But . . . "How did you know I speak English?"

A dimple appears when he smirks and points at me with his little plastic spatula-like spoon. "Because you're taking pictures of your food, which means not only that you speak English, but you're also American. Probably a blogger."

I click the lens cap back on and let the camera rest safely on my lap. "Well, of course now you know I'm American because you can hear that I don't have an accent. And I'm not a blogger."

I tried blogging last year, mostly to post some of the photos I was proud of, but I never got any followers, so I took the blog down. I keep my special photos to myself now.

"Oh, you have an accent." He takes another bite and leans back in his chair. "It's *American.* And northern, by the sound of it." He points at me with his spoon again. "Gelato's melting."

I look at my cup and gasp when I see how much is being wasted, dripping all down the side and making a puddle on the table. I quickly scrape the spoon along the edge before lifting it to my mouth.

My eyes close automatically, helping to block out all other senses but taste. And the green one is mint, not pistachio, thankfully. It's the softest, creamiest, most amazing flavor I've ever experienced. My tongue is cool, not only because the gelato is cold, but because of the mint itself. It floods my whole mouth then disappears down my throat. I need more.

I dip my spoon into the other flavor. "Ohhhh, wow this is good." I sigh.

"First timer?"

I swallow and nod, looking back at my table companion. "It's amazing."

"So, you're not a blogger. Are you a photographer then?"

"Hopefully one day."

"Oh," he says as he rubs his fingers over his dark stubble. I can hear it, scratchy like sandpaper. "How old are you?"

"Seventeen."

Suddenly I feel insecure, like he'll think I'm too young to bother with now. I shake the thought away and rescue another bite of gelato from the heat.

"You seem older than that," he says, somehow finished with his monster cup. He wads his napkin into a ball before plopping it in.

I smile and watch as the melted remains saturate the entire napkin. "Yeah, I've been told that before, actually."

Mom says it's the way I handle myself, especially around adults and strangers. I've been forced into more than my share of social situations where I was often the only child, so I learned to fit in to my surroundings.

"How old are you?" I ask.

"Eighteen. Just turned."

"Really, you seem . . . younger than that."

I did *not* just flirt with him.

He smiles, revealing mostly straight teeth. One of the top ones is a little crooked, but not in a hideous way. I kind of like it actually.

"Yeah, well, I—" He stops and his eyes shift behind me, wide in amusement.

I turn my head to find a couple straight out of the 1980s at the end of the gelato line. They're both sporting mullets and faded jeans. White sneakers. When I notice the matching red fanny packs, I have to look away.

"You should take a picture of that," he says, resting his forearms on the table.

"What?" I lean in closer and speak just above a whisper. "No way."

"Do it!" he insists. "Five euros." He digs into his pocket and clanks down five coins.

I sneak a peek at the unsuspecting couple. The man is wiping sweat off his face with a hanky. They're too close. I'd never get away with it.

"I can't," I say.

"Pansy."

With a grunt, I switch my camera on and set it to automatic. I raise it to my face and start to twist my upper body.

"No, wait!" he says. "You're doing it wrong."

I drop the camera to my lap and face him. "What?"

"You're too obvious. You need stealth. Watch and learn." He retrieves a small point-and-shoot camera from his pocket and aims it toward me. "Say cheese!" he says so loudly that I'm sure everyone around us is looking.

"Uh . . . cheese?"

"Done." He hits a few buttons and shows me the display screen.

There they are. Looked right at him too. Clever. But I can't let him win.

"Wow. That's pretty pixelated. What kind of setting do you have that on?"

He frowns. "It's just zoomed in."

"Oh." I reach to zoom out, but he pulls it away too fast. "What? Why can't I see? Did you actually take a picture of me or something?"

"Stealth." He shrugs and my cheeks turn pink. "Guess these are my winnings." The coins scrape across the table as he scoops them up to put in his pocket.

"You didn't even give me a chance to redeem myself," I defend.

"Excuses, excuses. Just admit I'm the better photographer." He laughs, standing to shoot his empty cup in the trash. "Finished?"

I nod and he tosses mine too. "Braver maybe, but better? Your camera doesn't have enough buttons."

His dimples reappear as he shoves his hands into the pockets of his navy-blue cargo shorts. "Well, thanks for letting me sit with you."

"Oh, sure. No problem." I slouch into my seat and wiggle my fingers in a low wave before reaching into my bag for the map from the hotel.

He still hasn't walked away. "Where you headed?"

"Not sure." I shrug. "I want to check out the Colosseum, but I'm sort of getting hungry."

He grips the back of the chair he'd sat in and leans on it. "You ate gelato before dinner too, huh?"

I shrug again. "When in Rome."

He laughs. "It's going to get dark soon. I'm not sure you should venture halfway across the city by yourself. Unless"—he looks around—"you're with your family or something."

No. My family sent me over here. All. By. Myself.

"Oh. Well, I planned on going alone."

He moves to stand next to me and points at the map. His hand lightly brushes against mine for the tiniest fraction of a second. "We're here, and the Colosseum is over here. There's no metro close, so it'll be a bit of a walk but definitely doable. I could go with you . . . if you want."

I look up at him to gauge if he's serious and I feel a little swirl in my stomach.

"I don't even know your name," I say.

"Oh, I'm sorry!" He takes a small step back and offers me his hand.

Our fingers are just about to touch when a girl's voice calls out and startles me. "Hey, Darren!"

The guy about to shake my hand turns his head in response.

A rail-thin girl strides over to us. She's wearing jean capris with a loose, purple sundress overtop, and several brass necklaces that dangle almost to her stomach. Bulky sunglasses perch high in the messy bleached-blond hair piled on top of her head.

"I'm Darren, and this is Nina," he says to me when she stops next to him.

Nina looks me over. "Hi." Her tone is friendly with an undercurrent of protectiveness.

"Hi," I respond, with maybe a little too much *I come in peace* worked in. "I'm Pippa."

"Pippa? Isn't that a cute name?" Nina squeaks, surprisingly genuine. She looks up at Darren and smiles, and my eyes follow hers to him.

"It's a great name," he agrees. There's his little twisted tooth again.

I've always thought my name was ridiculous, but if a guy can like it . . . My cheeks flush.

Darren clears his throat. "Pippa still hasn't seen the Colosseum. How do you feel about walking over there?" he asks Nina.

"Sure!" She turns toward him and holds out her palm. "But I want some gelato first."

Without missing a beat, he pulls a few coins out of his pocket and drops them in her palm.

"Thanks, doll," she says as she scampers off.

So he has a girlfriend. My reaction to this piece of information confuses me. Part of me is relieved—I feel like if he's got a girlfriend, the chances of him being a psycho trying to lure me away are slightly less. But another part of me is disappointed.

Oh, well. He's not Italian anyway.

NOTHING IS MORE OFF LIMITS THAN
YOUR BEST FRIEND'S CRUSH . . .
ESPECIALLY IF HE'S YOUR NEW COSTAR!

if only

Amy Finnegan

NOT
IN
THE
SCRIPT

COMING
SOON!

BLOOMSBURY

*Read on for a glimpse at another romance filled with
paparazzi, on-set drama, and a delicious love triangle.*

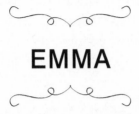

EMMA

"*Celebrity Seeker* claims that I'm dating Troy again," I say as I skim the pages of the gossip magazine. Tabloids are scattered like fall leaves all over Rachel's bedroom, and I want to rake them up and stuff them into trash bags. "How stupid do they think I am?"

I haven't talked to Troy since he shattered my car window three months ago. Rachel doesn't know anything about that, though. No one does, and I have to keep it that way.

"I'd feel bad for you, Emma, but some of us don't have any guys to ignore." Rachel has her back to me, admiring the collection of men who cover her otherwise lavender walls. Most of the space is taken up by carefully cut out magazine pages featuring a male model she calls The Bod. "And worse, the only guy I'm dying to date doesn't know I exist. Literally."

"I doubt he's worth dying for," I say. "If a boy looks like he belongs in a museum, there's a pretty good chance his head is solid marble."

Rachel huffs at me, offended, as if she actually knows him. Or even his name.

I leave her bouncy desk chair—great for girls with energy to burn—to study a close-up of The Bod's face. "At the very least," I go on with a teasing tone, "those puffy lips are airbrushed."

Chancing a peek at Rachel, I find her bright-green eyes narrowed at me. "You know," she says, "for someone who's on *People* magazine's Most Beautiful Young Celebrities list, you're awfully critical of beautiful people."

I suppose being my best friend for over a decade gives her the right to call me out on things like this. And Rachel is all about straight talk and honesty, which is usually a good thing.

My life doesn't always feel genuine, even when cameras aren't rolling.

Whenever I return to my hometown in Fayetteville, Arkansas, I expect the world to somehow seem real again, but work still has a way of taking over. Today especially, because a full five minutes hasn't passed without me checking my e-mail. The final details for the new TV series I'm starting next month are being sent out today, including the casting choices.

The scent of coconut-and-lime body spray wafts toward me. Rachel snaps her fingers in front of my face. "Are you even listening?"

Yes and no. She's been going on about the endless charms of her paperweight soul mate. "All I'm saying is that guys who look like The Bod are usually the most overrated gimmicks on the planet," I tell her. "And crappy boyfriend material. Trust me."

I hear a screen door squeak open, and a canary-like chirp belonging to Rachel's mom instantly echoes in the house. Trina enters the room and says, "Oh, Emma honey, have *we* got a big surprise!"

For as long as I can remember, Trina has dressed like she's forty-going-on-sixteen. At the moment she's in black skinny jeans and a plum tee with a glittery fleur-de-lis stretched way too tight over her five-thousand-dollar chest. Trina's curly platinum hair matches her daughter's, but everything about Rachel's beauty is perfectly natural.

"You're just gonna die!" Trina adds.

My mother is right behind Trina and shoots her a *please stop* look, but I seem to be the only one who notices. Typical for her, Mom is wearing a white button-down shirt and gray tweed slacks, looking like she walked out of a Neiman Marcus window display. She wouldn't be caught dead in Trina's leopard print stilettos. But despite being polar opposites, they've been going out for regular lunches since Rachel and I first met in a community acting class.

I sometimes wonder if Mom only does it to stay on the good side of a careless gossip who might be too close to me. Or maybe Mom just wants to keep up on what's *really* going on in my personal life. She likely gets more from Trina, via Rachel, than she does from me.

Trina is still grinning so widely that every tooth in her mouth is showing, but my mom's smile seems fake, and her lashes are batting way too fast to be simple blinks. "I just heard from the studio," she says.

I only stare at her for a second. "But . . . why wasn't I on the e-mail list?"

"I'll forward you a copy, Emma. I always do."

That's not the point, and she knows it. I had asked her to tell the studio to put me on the direct list, and she obviously didn't. Like a lot of parents in this business, my mom became my manager when I landed my first big job, so *everything* goes through her. But now that I'm finally an official adult, I can hire a new management team if I want to, a team who would at least agree that I should know—before the rest of the world—what's going on in my career. Like me, Mom must realize this isn't working anymore, but she hasn't even mentioned the possibility of a new manager, like it isn't something I'd consider anyway.

As if she could never imagine me making a mature decision without her.

Mom tacks on a sigh. "We should head home so we can discuss this casting."

"I want to stay. Just tell me what the e-mail says."

"I'm dying to know too," Rachel adds. "We've been waiting all day."

Trina whispers something to Rachel, then Rachel looks at me with her mouth half open, her eyes bulging. "Holy crap, Emma! You're gonna FREAK!"

Perfect. Now even Rachel knows before I do.

"Can we borrow this room for a minute?" I ask.

Trina and Rachel appear disappointed by the request but finally step into the hallway, whispering again. My mom shuts the bedroom door and pulls out her phone. "I had hoped we were past this nonsense," she mutters, "but you won't believe who's playing—"

I snatch the phone from her hand, open the e-mail from the studio, and read out loud. "Executive Producer Steve McGregor will launch the production of *Coyote Hills* in Tucson, Arizona, the second week of July . . . table read . . . camera tests . . . I'll go back to that later . . . Okay, here it is: one male lead is still in negotiations." Ugh. This is practically code for *casting problems.* "The remaining cast is as follows: Eden will be played by Emma Taylor. The role of Kassidy will be played by Kimmi Weston." I have no idea who Kimmi is, so I glance at my mom before going on. She's never heard of her either. "And the role of Bryce will be played by Brett Crawford."

I drop the phone.

I want to stomp on it. Scream at it!

Or possibly hug it and jump up and down.

I'm not sure which yet.

"You see?" Mom says. "This is why I wanted to tell you privately."

My arms are as limp as overcooked fettuccini, but I manage to scoop up the phone. "Okay, yeah. Him," I say, going for indifference. "A bit of a shock, but whatever."

Mom puts a hand on her hip. *Here we go.* "Emma, you know how tired I am of dealing with high-publicity romances," she begins, in full-blown managerial mode. "The last two years have been ridiculous, putting out one tabloid fire after another. You're at a crossroads here and have a chance to prove yourself as a serious actress. Brett Crawford is the worst sort of boy for you to get involved with, so don't even consider dating him."

Does she really think *I* would want to go through all that crap again? On-set romances are usually total disasters, and not just for me. Until last spring I was on a primetime drama that, despite sky-high ratings, was cancelled due to conflict on the set. I played the president's daughter, but the actor playing the president was caught having a real-life relationship with the actress who played the first lady—and unfortunately, she also happened to be our executive producer's wife. It wasn't pretty.

And it eventually shut the entire show down.

That was when Steve McGregor, the do-it-all executive producer/creator/director of *Coyote Hills*, called my agent to ask if he could meet with me to discuss his new project. It was the very day the cancellation of *The First Family* was announced, and I haven't received a bigger compliment in the six years of my career.

McGregor is responsible for more hit dramas than any producer in television—his shows don't even require pilots. I think his methods are brilliant, but some people say he's a nutcase. For one thing, he's already slated to direct about one-third of the first season, which either means the guy really is insane or he plans to live with a caffeine drip attached to his arm. McGregor is also notoriously secretive about who he's considering for his cast or I would have already known about Brett. And he rarely takes time to screen-test a pair of actors—who he's already familiar with—for chemistry. But I've worked with enough cinematic geniuses to know there's no use questioning them. You just go along.

"Listen, Mom," I say, trying to hide the likelihood that the pizza I had for lunch is about to land on her Jimmy Choo pumps. "This isn't a big deal. I had a silly celebrity crush on Brett when I was, like, eight." Well, it started about then, and went on and on. But his growing reputation as a guy who never commits, just loves whoever he's with at the moment, has definitely dampened my enthusiasm. "That's ancient history. I'm totally over him."

Totally may be pushing it. I might still watch his movies, a lot, and rewind certain parts that I think he's especially amazing in. But is it so wrong that I think he's the best actor of my generation? Isn't it natural that I would be attracted to someone with so much talent?

Mom gives me a thin, cynical smile. "I noticed just this

morning that your laptop wallpaper is yet another picture of Brett Crawford."

Yeah, well, about that . . . I also just like to *look* at him.

"The only time it's been otherwise in the last ten years," Mom goes on, "is when you've been dating some other Hollywood hotshot who thought nothing of dragging your name through the mud."

Why did she have to bring *them* into this? "It isn't my fault that they all cheated on me. *I* didn't do anything wrong."

Mom's icy expression melts a little, and I realize I rarely see this softer look on her face anymore. She has brown eyes, mine are blue, but we share the same dark hair and small-framed bodies. I've never felt like she's forced me into a life I don't want—I'm the one who got the lead in a first-grade play and begged her to let me become a real actress—but it feels as if she sometimes forgets that I'm not just a client.

It's all business, all the time.

"I know that," Mom says. "And your dad and your closest friends know that. But the majority of the world looks at a girl who dates this same type of guy over and over, as someone who has very poor judgment. It just can't happen again."

How could she possibly think I pick losers on purpose?

When I first met Troy, who was my costar during the last season of *The First Family*, he was always smiling, laughing, joking around with me, surprising me with flowers or a dinner overlooking the ocean. But it isn't exactly easy dating professional actors—guys who can fake their way through anything.

I look my mom square in the eyes and say, "I get it, okay? I'm totally done with Hollywood guys. Can we move on now?"

Someone sneezes. Rachel and Trina are just outside the door

and have probably been there this entire time, listening. Mom breathes a familiar sigh of irritation. "We'll talk more when you get home," she says. "And perhaps you can find a new wallpaper for your laptop?"

I nod and return her phone. "Don't worry. I'll be . . ." Fine is what I'd intended to say, but a vision of Brett Crawford sitting next to me in a cast chair—with his perfect surfer tan, blond hair that always falls in front of his eyes, and a smile that puts a humming-bird in my stomach—enters my mind, and I can't speak.

"You'll be *amazing*," Mom says with a squeeze of my shoulder. "Steve McGregor didn't even consider another actress for this part, and he always knows what he's doing. You just need to focus on your career, not boys."

Mom leaves the room, and Rachel soon takes her place. She shuts the door again and says, "Are you freaking out or what? *Brett Crawford?* This is fate!"

"It's *ill*-fated, you mean." I collapse into her bed pillows and throw one over my face. I've had several chances to meet Brett. A few times, I've even been in the same room as him. But besides the fact that he's more than two years older and would have only thought of me as a silly little girl before now, I've intentionally avoided Brett because I don't want to know the real him. "I have a perfectly happy relationship with my laptop wallpaper version of Brett Crawford, thank you very much."

As things are, we never fight, he never cheats on me, and he doesn't . . . scare me.

"Brett was in television for the first several years of his career, so why would he want to come back?" I add. "He's been doing *great* in big-budget movies. He should stay where he is."

Rachel plops into her desk chair. "Don't you keep up with anything? It's amazing how much more I know about your world than you do."

It's not such a bad thing that Rachel always knows more gossip than I do; Hollywood is practically her religion. When we met, Rachel had already been doing commercials since she was a baby in a Downy-soft blanket, so she was quick to make herself my mentor. But a few years later, when we were twelve, we both went to an open audition for what turned out to be an Oscar-winning film, and I got the part.

It was a lucky break. Right time, right place, right look.

Since then, I've done whatever I could to get Rachel auditions for other major projects, but nothing has worked out. And tension builds with every failed attempt. A few months ago she straight out told me, "How did this even happen? You have *everything* I want."

Why doesn't she get that I wish she had it all too?

No matter how different things sometimes feel between us, though, one thing stays the same: Rachel is the only friend I have who's been with me all along—the only friend who keeps my feet planted firmly in the dark, rich soil of Arkansas. Even when I'm dressed from head to toe in Prada, with red carpet beneath me and cameras flashing from every other direction, Rachel is a constant reminder of where I came from. Who I really am.

I blow the silver fringe from her pillow off my face. "Are you talking about Brett's girl issues?" I ask. "Because, crazy enough, being a player only seems to *help* a guy's career."

"But it's more than just that," Rachel says. "According to insiders, Brett's been a pain to work with on his last few films. He misses call times and keeps the cast and crew waiting for hours." Rachel sounds like a newscaster as she presents a tattered tabloid as evidence. "Critics say he's lost his passion for acting, that he'll be nothing but a washed-up child star if he doesn't do something quick to redeem himself. So his management team must think television is his best bet. It's worked for a ton of other actors."

I've read some of this, but not all. "Everyone knows what a great actor Brett is—he's been nominated for major awards since he was *five,*" I say. "He's probably just burned out, and McGregor is smart enough to realize he'll push through it."

"Yeah, I guess I can see that. But back to the girl issues," Rachel replies and tacks on a sly smile. "You know what Brett's problem is? He just hasn't dated the *right* girl yet."

I toss a pillow at her. "The last thing I want to be is Brett Crawford's next 'throwaway party favor,' so don't look at *me,*" I say, then I make a silent promise to put soap in my mouth for quoting a tabloid. Reporters tell plenty of lies about my own life, so I question everything I read, but I've seen enough myself to know that every once in a while they're surprisingly dead-on. In their pursuit of a quick, juicy story to sell, however, gossipmongers often miss the details that could *really* damage someone. "It's just that this is all sort of sad," I go on. "Brett has always been someone safe for me to crush on, but now—"

Rachel cuts me off with laughter. "Oh, please! You *know* what's gonna happen. Brett will fall head over heels in love and change his whole life to be with you. So just flirt a little and see where things go."

"No way," I reply. She might understand if I told her how bad things got with Troy, but I can't take the chance of Rachel telling

Trina, who would go straight to my mom. Then Mom would freak out even more about me living on my own in Arizona, which is something I've had to fight for every day for the past few months. "I just need to get over Brett before we start working together. That's all. Or he'll be . . . well, a bit of a distraction."

"More like a tall, beautiful problem with a killer smile." Rachel turns back to her wall to swoon over The Bod in a western-themed cologne ad for Armani. "I can only imagine how distracted I'd be if I ever worked with *my* dream guy. Distracted by his perfectly toned arms, and his amazing green eyes, and his luscious mocha hair, and . . . gosh, I better not talk him up *too* much, or you'll want to start a collection of your own. But The Bod is all mine, got it?"

I probably sound just as ridiculous as Rachel does when I talk about Brett—I mean, when I *used* to talk about Brett—but I laugh anyway. "Yep, he's all yours," I reply. "Down to his last curly eyelash."

I have to agree with Rachel on one thing, though: The Bod, whoever he is, makes leather cowboy chaps look seriously hot.

Teen FIC HUBBARD

Hubbard, Mandy
Fool me twice : an If
 only novel

11/20/14

NOV 2 4 2014